MISSION BRIEFING

You are Terry Morton, and your interest in electronics has led you into big trouble. Dangerous spies have broken into your uncle's electronics factory and stolen plans for a top secret security robot.

What will you do?

The spies ~~~~~~ pre~~~~~~~~~~~ eir getaway w~~~~ ~~~~~~~~~~ ~~~d-ing you an~~ ~~~~~~~~~~ ~~e in a wareho~~~~ ~~~~~~ ~~oice:

1) If you ~~~~~~ to trick your captors into opening the door and then make a run for it, turn to page 63.

2) If you want to use some nearby electrical wire as a rope and try to escape through the window, turn to page 103.

3) If you choose to try to hook into the telephone lines and send a message for help, turn to page 124.

Whichever path you pick, you are sure to find adventure as you turn the pages of **ROBBERS AND ROBOTS**

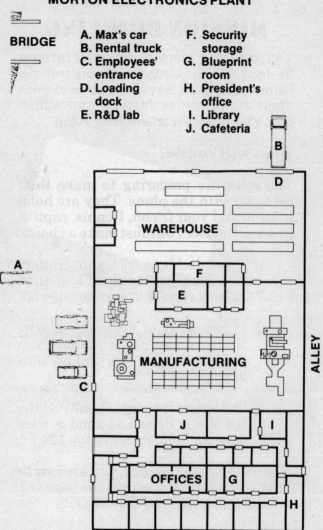

MORTON ELECTRONICS PLANT

BRIDGE

A. Max's car
B. Rental truck
C. Employees' entrance
D. Loading dock
E. R&D lab

F. Security storage
G. Blueprint room
H. President's office
I. Library
J. Cafeteria

WAREHOUSE

F

E

MANUFACTURING

J

I

OFFICES

G

H

ALLEY

ROBBERS
and ROBOTS

BY MIKE CARR

Cover Art by Elmore
Interior Art by Vernon Posey

TSR Inc.

For Gordon and Shirley,
who did a good job

ROBBERS AND ROBOTS
©copyright 1983 TSR Hobbies, Inc.
All Rights Reserved.

Distributed to the book trade in the United States by Random
House, Inc. and in Canada by Random House of Canada, Ltd.
Distributed in the United Kingdom by TSR (UK), Ltd.
Distributed to the toy and hobby trade by regional distributors.

DUNGEONS & DRAGONS, ENDLESS QUEST, TOP SECRET,
and PICK A PATH TO ADVENTURE are trademarks owned
by TSR Hobbies, Inc.

D&D is a registered trademark owned by TSR Hobbies, Inc.

First Printing: July, 1983
Printed in the United States of America
Library of Congress Catalog Card Number: 83-50049

ISBN: 0-88038-036-5

9 8 7 6 5 4 3 2 1

TSR Hobbies, Inc.   TSR Hobbies (UK), Ltd.
P.O. Box 756   The Mill, Rathmore Road
Lake Geneva, WI 53147   Cambridge CB1 4AD
                           United Kingdom

ou are about to set off on an adventure in which YOU will meet many dangers—and face many decisions. YOUR choices will determine how the story turns out. So be careful . . . you must choose wisely!

Do not read this book from beginning to end! Instead, as you are faced with a decision, follow the instructions and keep turning to the pages where your choices lead you until you come to an end. At any point, YOUR choice could bring success—or disaster!

You can read ROBBERS AND ROBOTS many times, with many different results, so if you make an unwise choice, go back to the beginning and start again.

Good luck on YOUR adventure!

In this story, you are Terry Morton, a young person with an avid interest in electronics, at the moment completely unaware of the dangers you are about to face. You, your dog, Rusty, and your friend, Dennis Frost, are enjoying a Saturday morning walk on the way to your uncle's robot factory as the story begins . . . .

"Your very own robot!" Dennis exclaims. "I still find that hard to believe."

Your golden retriever, Rusty, cocks his head to the side and looks at you as if he, too, finds it hard to believe.

"Well, it's not really mine, but I did help build it—with lots of help, of course."

"I think it's neat that your Uncle Sidney runs a robot company. You're pretty lucky, you know. My uncle owns a laundromat."

There's a trace of envy in Dennis's voice. He kicks a stone off the sidewalk and watches it until it stops rolling.

"Morton Electronics isn't just a robot company," you explain. "It makes lots of electronic things. I've really learned a lot by spending the summer here with my uncle. He let me see all the work they do. And then Bob Gladding, the research manager, offered to show me how to build a robot.

"He was making one called Gert, so I built one just like it and called mine Bert. Wait till you see 'em! I'm glad they're finished, so I can show you how they work today."

Dennis shakes his head in wonder. "I don't know how you do it, Terry. To me, electronics is a mystery. But you're really good at it."

"It's just a knack I have, I guess. I've always been interested in electronics. And I read lots of books about it, too."

"Don't you ever get tired of it? I mean, doesn't taking apart telephones and stuff get boring after a while?" It's obvious Dennis doesn't share your fascination for the subject.

"No, not at all," you reply. "Everything is a little bit different inside, and you never know what you're going to find until you open it up. You remember that video game I fixed for you last week? It was like solving a puzzle."

"Well, you acted pretty puzzled when I beat you at it after you fixed it!"

You knew Dennis wouldn't be able to resist reminding you of that. He may not know much about electronics, but he sure is a wizard at electronic games.

You are thinking about this as you wait for the traffic to clear before crossing the busy street you've come to. Rusty waits patiently at the curb for the right moment, then crosses with you, his coat glistening like gold in the morning sun.

"Can your uncle's robots really zap somebody?" Dennis asks.

"They sure can," you explain. "And pretty good, too. But security robots are still experimental. These will move around a building, following a chemical track on the floor, or they can be maneuvered by remote control with a hand controller like this one." You fish in your pants pocket and pull out what looks like a tiny pocket calculator.

Dennis examines it with interest. "It's so small. What are all these buttons for?"

Taking the controller back from Dennis, you point out different buttons as you explain.

"This one turns the robot on or off by remote

control. These buttons make it move or turn in different directions. This little screen shows where and how far away someone—maybe a burglar—is when the robot's sensors detect his body heat. And these other buttons make the robot do other things, like flashing a bright light, sounding an alarm, or using its arms to grab something."

"What about the zapper?"

"It's called a Taser device. It shoots out a little dart with a wire attached, and it gives off a pretty good shock. It'll buzz a guy for a second, and then he won't be able to move for a while until it wears off. But he's okay later." As you start to put the controller back into your pocket, Dennis pulls something from his.

"Here's what I've been working on this week," he says proudly. He holds up a small bottle filled with a pink-colored liquid.

Knowing Dennis's love for chemistry, you are curious. But before you can ask, he tells you. "It's a liquid that produces knockout gas when you expose it to the air."

"C'mon, Dennis, that's too much. Even your new chemistry set doesn't have enough stuff to make something like that!"

"You're right," Dennis says, "but having a big brother who's a chemistry major at the university helps a lot."

Now you begin to take him seriously. "Does it really work?"

"Well, I think it will. I thought we could try it out on Rusty," Dennis says with a laugh. At the mention of his name, Rusty stops and turns, ears peaked. Dennis leans down and pats the dog. "Just kidding, fella," he says reassuringly. He looks back up at you and continues. "Actually, I thought we could try it out on some of those muskrats down by the river."

"Yeah, there's usually some of them on those cement sewer outlets down the hill from my uncle's plant. We can corner a couple and try out your knockout gas after I show you the robots. It'll be fun!"

As you cross the railroad tracks, Dennis abruptly changes the subject. "When do you have to leave for home?" Suddenly you don't feel so good anymore.

"Next week, on Tuesday. School starts the week after that. But I'm sure not looking forward to it."

"Why not?" Dennis asks. "Don't you like your school?"

"Oh, it's okay, I guess, especially since I'll be president of the computer club this year. But I don't have many real friends there. In fact, even though we just met this summer, you're the best friend I have."

"Hey, thanks, Terry. You've been a lot of fun to have around. It's too bad you don't live around here. But don't worry about school. You'll make more friends. Sometimes it takes a while. And having a few really good friends is more important than being popular with everybody."

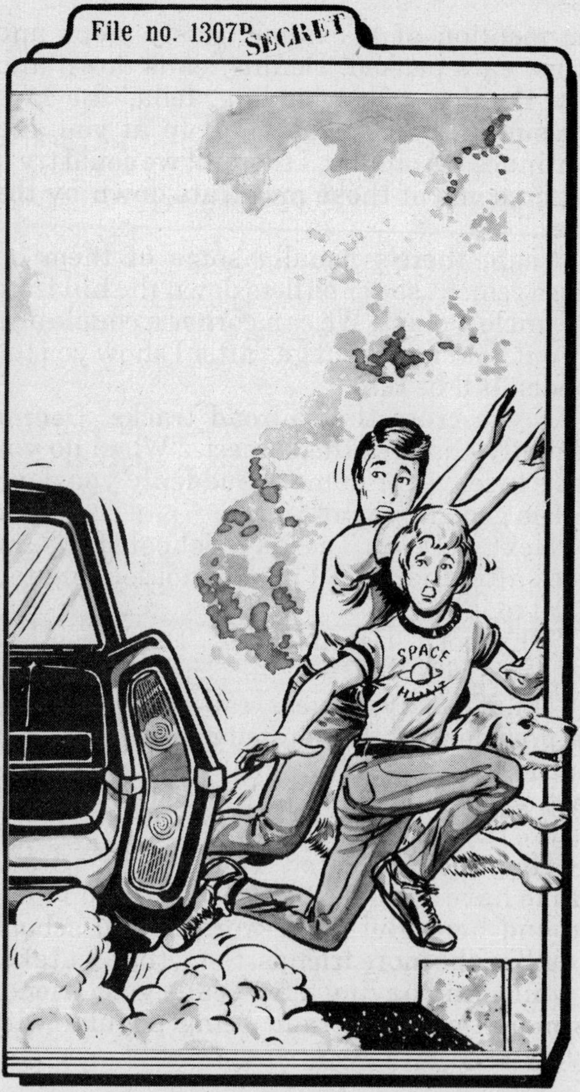
File no. 1307P
SECRET
SPACE
HUNT

You step off the curb of another street near your uncle's factory.

HONNNK!

You jump in reaction to the blaring horn as a big black sedan rockets around the corner. In horror, you watch as it misses Rusty by inches. Then as you jump aside, the car swerves and flashes past you.

"Outta the way, Terry!" the driver shouts out the window at you.

He meant to scare you! Your shock turns to anger as you realize who the driver is.

"Max Kimball!" you sputter. "He works at the Morton Electronics plant with Bob Gladding and my uncle."

"What a jerk!"

"You said it! He's been mean and unfriendly all summer. He says he hates kids and dogs both. He even kicked Rusty one time. Lately, he's been sore at Bob and my uncle because Bob's robot design was accepted and his wasn't. He made a robot called Bruno, and for months all anyone heard was how great it was. Then when it didn't get approved by my uncle, Max got real mad at everybody."

You pause. Something doesn't make sense. Then you realize what it is. "Wait a minute. Why's Max going to the plant? He's supposed to be on vacation in Hawaii!"

You and Dennis discuss the puzzle as you walk the last few blocks to the Morton Electronics plant. Crossing the bridge over the river, you have a full view of the building. A large parking lot slopes down toward the riverbank. Because it's usually full of cars during the week, it looks pretty empty on a Saturday.

Approaching the end of the bridge, you realize that something doesn't look quite right at the plant.

"Hold it a minute, Dennis."

"What's up?" he asks.

"I don't know," you reply uncertainly, "but something's wrong. Let's wait here for a minute." You motion toward a telephone booth alongside a cement piling at the end of the bridge. Rusty waits patiently while you and Dennis peer over the top of the cement.

"Look!" you say, pointing at the nearly empty parking lot. "That's Max standing by his car out toward the back of the lot."

"What's he doing, Terry? Is that a walkie-talkie he's holding?"

You study Max as he leans against his car. He's a large, overweight man with a bald spot on top of his head. He seems to be talking into something in his hand as he glances about nervously.

"I don't know for sure, but it looks like it," you say to Dennis.

You recognize three other cars in the parking lot. One belongs to Bob Gladding, the research manager. The other two belong to Milt Davis and Ed Segal, the security guards at the plant. "Those other three cars would normally be here on a Saturday, but I sure

don't know what Max is doing here!" you tell Dennis.

Looking around the corner of the building, you see a truck backed into the loading dock. "Express Truck Rental" is painted on the side.

"I've never seen that truck at the loading dock here before. The company has its own trucks. And there usually aren't any shipments on Saturdays anyway."

"Do you think something's wrong? Maybe we'd better call the cops," Dennis says.

"I don't know if anything's wrong," you reply slowly. "But I do wonder what's going on. We'd feel pretty silly if we called the police and it turned out there was a perfectly reasonable explanation. I could call my uncle, but he won't be home until tonight. Maybe we should check it out."

1) If you think you should go ask Max what is going on, turn to page 152.

2) If you think you should stay hidden and watch what Max does, then check outside the building, turn to page 115.

The warehouse is a large area, with row upon row of shipping boxes piled high.

"What if we find someone?" Dennis whispers. The question is a good one—and one you haven't thought about until now.

"I don't know. But I'm sure there's something going on, and we've got to find out what." You try to sound confident, but inside you feel anything but.

Trying to keep quiet, you look up and down each aisle, but nothing seems to be out of place. There is no sign of anyone. It seems almost too quiet. Rusty sniffs at some of the boxes, but he doesn't seem to notice anything unusual, either. Maybe nothing's going on, after all. Maybe it's just your imagination.

1) If you want to hide and wait to see if anyone comes into the warehouse, turn to page 57.

2) If you want to check the security storage room, where valuable parts are kept, turn to page 42.

As quietly as possible, you and Dennis and Rusty make your way through the warehouse. You move toward the manufacturing area, keeping hidden as much as you can behind rows of boxes.

The large door leading out of the warehouse is open, and you peek into the area where products are assembled.

"Wow!" gasps Dennis as he looks out over the large machine-filled room. "Is this where they make everything?"

"Yeah, those are assembly lines," you reply. "They make radios and computer parts here."

You continue on, crouching behind the machines. You have to keep urging Dennis on because he becomes absorbed in each machine you pass. Rusty follows quietly, occasionally pausing to sniff at a machine.

You make your way through the assembly area to a metal door. "This goes to the offices," you whisper.

You turn the doorknob and slowly pull the door toward you, looking through the widening crack. The coast seems clear, so you open the door wide enough to slip through.

"Let's check the halls first," you whisper to Dennis as you start slowly down the corridor. "My uncle's office is over this way." When the hall turns a corner, you stop and listen carefully. There doesn't seem to be anyone around.

You move on quietly, listening as you go. The only sound is the tap of Rusty's nails on the tile floor. As you make your way down the corridor, you pass the company library and the vice-president's office.

You come to another door, and you grab the knob, expecting it to be locked. When the knob turns, you know you may have found something. You turn to Dennis.

"This is a security area. The door's always supposed to be locked."

"What's in there?" Dennis asks.

"All the important offices, the computer room, and the blueprint files. My uncle's office is just on the other side of this door."

"Do you want to go through there?"

"Yeah. I think we might find something."

"Be careful, Terry," Dennis pleads.

You turn the knob again and slowly push the door open. You notice a big piece of tape covering the latch, which you point out to Dennis as you move through the doorway. He holds the door open to let Rusty through, then quietly eases it closed.

When you see the door to your uncle's office, you get another surprise. A key is in the doorknob.

"There's a key in the door!" you whisper.

"Does it belong to your uncle?"

"I don't know. This is strange."

Quietly you open the door and look around the office. No one is there and everything looks undisturbed. You ease back out and close the door, leaving the key where it was.

You step quietly down the corridor. Just as you're about to turn the corner, you hear a noise ahead of you—a sound like paper rustling. Rusty hears it, too, and his ears perk up.

You signal Dennis to wait behind you. Slowly, one step at a time, you quietly turn the corner and move along the wall of the corridor toward the sound. Ahead, you can see a door open on the right side of the hallway. It's the blueprint file room, and someone is shuffling papers around in there! Cautiously you edge closer.

You pause for a moment just outside the doorway, then tip your head just enough to see into the room. A man with his back to you stands beside a table, looking through papers and drawings. He's a large man, and from the gray trench coat he's wearing, you know that he's not someone who works at your uncle's company!

1) If you want to sneak up behind the intruder and, with Dennis's help, jump him, turn to page 48.

2) If you want to use Dennis's bottle of knockout gas on the man, turn to page 38.

You and Dennis struggle futilely as the men tie you up. "Don't be afraid, Terry!" are Dennis's last words before a gag is placed in his mouth. But the expression on his face betrays his fear. You don't have any time to reply before a dirty, greasy rag is stuffed in your own mouth.

The men place each of you inside separate video game packing crates. Fear grips you as you hear them nail the shell shut with you inside! You hear tapping on the side of the crate as you feel your tiny prison being pushed into the cargo container.

"See you later, kid! Enjoy the flight." Max's evil laugh echoes in your ears long after the heavy door of the cargo container is slammed shut.

Soon you feel the container being moved. It must be on its way to the airport. In the darkness of your prison, you wonder if Dennis is as scared as you are.

It isn't long before you feel the container, with you inside, being loaded aboard an airplane. You try to yell, but there's just no way you can do it with the suffocating gag in your mouth.

You hear the jet engines start up. The noise is deafening, but there's nothing you can do about it. You realize that this may be the end for you.

The plane taxis down the runway, then turns and pauses. All of a sudden, the noise of the engines becomes unbearable and you feel the plane start to roll forward. It's going to take off!

As the plane climbs higher and higher, your helplessness grows. Tears pour down your face as you think of the home and family you'll never see again. The chilling cold seeps into your every muscle until you feel your body slipping away into a long, deep sleep. . . .

THE END

You, Dennis, and Rusty leave the warehouse quietly, squeezing back out the way you came in. You try to stay out of sight until you can get to the telephone booth on the bridge. You're nervous as you dial the 911 emergency number and ask for the police.

When the police dispatcher comes on the line, you tell her what you've seen. She says a patrol car will check it out. You wait on the bridge, keeping an eye on Max.

In a few minutes, three men come out of the building. You and Dennis look at each other, surprised. Who are they, and what were they doing inside? You watch as they close the loading dock door and get into the truck. Then Max gets into his car and drives out of the parking lot, with the truck following him. You feel helpless as you watch them drive away.

The police seem to take forever to come, even though it's only fifteen minutes or so. When they arrive, you tell them everything you've seen, and they approach the building.

When no one comes to the door, they ask the dispatcher to call on the telephone to see if anyone answers. But there is no answer, even though Bob's, Milt's, and Ed's cars are parked in the lot.

Finally they call the local night security service. In twenty minutes a man comes to unlock the doors.

Once inside, the police and the security man find Bob, Ed, and Milt tied up in the storage room. They're all right, but the robot models and all of the blueprints have been stolen. When you realize what has happened, you can't help feel that you should have done something else to help prevent the theft. Dennis tries to reassure you, and Bob says he'll help you build another robot if Bert isn't recovered. But you know it'll never be the same.

Fortunately, using the information you gave about Max and the rental van, the police arrest him at the airport that same night as he tries to board a flight out of the country.

When Max goes to trial several months later, you return to testify against him. Even on his way to prison, Max never tells where the robots and the blueprints are. You will always wonder if you might have saved Bert and Gert by doing things differently.

THE END

"I can use my robot against them!"

"Are you sure, Terry?"

"Sure. Just watch!" You press a button on your hand controller, and Bert comes to life with a loud HUMMM. The two men turn to look. Pressing buttons quickly, you move Bert toward the first man. His look of surprise almost makes you laugh out loud.

"Get him, Terry!" Dennis whispers.

As Bert advances, the man backs up, step by step. When he can move no farther, he gasps in astonishment as Bert reaches out and grabs him. You chuckle as Bert's monotone voice speaks one of the standard messages you programmed into him: "You are now my captive, human. Do not try to escape."

As you expected, the man tries to escape anyway. He struggles to free himself from Bert's viselike grasp. Again you press a button, and this time the small, dartlike Taser device shoots out and into the man. There's a quick buzz, and the agent's body goes limp in Bert's arms. You make Bert release the man, and he crumples to the floor.

"Wow!" Dennis exclaims.

All this time you've heard the other man speaking frantically into his hand-held radio, probably calling Max. After seeing his comrade's fate, he is frozen with astonishment.

You move Bert around the body on the floor, then toward the second man. His eyes almost pop out of his head, and he turns and runs for the other door. He's escaping!

"C'mon! Let's go after get him!" you shout, springing from your hiding place. Dennis quickly follows you to the lab door. The man is running out the other door just as you enter and put Bert on automatic pursuit.

Obeying your command, Bert pursues the man. With a series of rapid clicks, he's out the door and hot on the man's trail.

You and Dennis make your way through the lab and out the other door. You see Bert treading toward the warehouse entrance. The man looks back quickly, then darts through the door.

You reach the warehouse to see Bert suddenly stop in an aisle. On your special controller screen, you see the flashing dot that shows Bert still has the man in range of his sensors. But where is he?

"Up there, Terry!" Dennis shouts. You look where he's pointing. That explains it! The man has climbed up high on a pile of boxes so Bert can't follow. He's cornered!

As you're figuring out how to get the man down, you hear Rusty let out a sharp bark and Dennis shout, "Oh, no!" You turn and look back toward the doorway to the manufacturing area.

You hear a humming noise, and you know right away that you're in trouble. Then the shiny black shape of Bruno, Max's robot, rolls ominously through the doorway. Its giant claw flexes, as if feeling for you.

"Ha, ha!" Max laughs evilly. "Now we'll

find out whose robot is best, kid! Your piece of junk will never stand up to this monster!" It's going to be a fight!

You take Bert off automatic pursuit and turn him to face Bruno. Max stops his menacing black robot and glares at you.

"I've got a surprise for you kids," he says and takes out two sets of headphones from a compartment in Bruno's back. He tosses one up to the man on the pile of boxes and puts the other over his ears.

"What's he up to, Terry?" asks Dennis.

"I don't know," you say, puzzled.

There's no sense in waiting for Max to make a move, so you raise Bert's arms and advance him toward Bruno. The fight is on!

Max just stands there, laughing. You see him turn a dial on his controller, and suddenly Rusty starts to whine and run in circles. You try to figure out what's happening. Max turns the dial again and continues to laugh. But Max's laughter isn't the only sound you hear. . . .

All at once you hear a high-pitched squeal, like the sound a television set makes when it's turned on, only a hundred times louder. It's coming from Bruno!

You try to ignore the piercing sound and command Bert to attack, but Max turns the dial once more, and the sound grows to an unbearable crescendo. You try to get Rusty to go after Max, but Rusty's gone, driven off by the painful noise in his ears.

Dennis holds his hands over his ears and crouches down, as if to escape the unbearable sound. You cover your ears, too, but nothing seems to help. Your ears hurt . . . your head hurts . . . your brain hurts. Sobbing, you drop the controller.

That's what Max was counting on. He grabs you as the other man jumps down and seizes Dennis. Still the noise bombards you. It's the worst sound you've ever heard!

"Turn it off! Please! Turn it off!" you shout. Nothing else matters except stopping the pain!

Max pushes you against the wall, a look of scorn on his face. Then he turns the dial. It takes several seconds before you realize that the shrill sound has stopped. Your ears continue to ring with an echo of that horrible noise, but at least you can take your hands away. Max and the man peel off their headphones and push you and Dennis toward the storage room in the warehouse.

"You kids didn't expect Bruno's little sonic blast trick, did you? Well, hear no evil, see no evil! Ha, ha!" Max gloats.

As you near the storage room door, he takes a key from his pocket and unlocks the door. The door swings open, and there on the floor are Bob Gladding, Milt Davis, and Ed Segal, all tied up and gagged.

"You can join your friends here, Terry. They're probably getting lonely!" Max pushes you to the floor and ties and gags you. Dennis

struggles to get loose, but the other man easily overpowers him, and soon he joins you.

As Max leaves he says, "It's too bad you all had to get in our way. But don't worry. We'll be far away very soon now!"

With that taunting farewell, Max turns out the light and slams the door, surrounding you in blackness.

Even though your friends are beside you, you still feel all alone in the darkness. You struggle to free yourself, but it's no use. There's nothing to do but wait.

The hours pass slowly. Your body becomes stiff and sore, but there's nothing you can do about it. When you think about Max getting away with this, it makes you angry.

After what seems like days, the door opens and the night security guard releases all of you. You find out you've been tied up about five hours.

The police come and the five of you tell them your stories. When Uncle Sid arrives at the plant, he's in a state of shock. Bob Gladding tries to reassure him, but you can tell that what's happened has really hurt your uncle's company.

In a few days, you go back home to start school. You keep hoping Max will be caught, but he never is. If only you'd done something different, maybe he'd never have gotten away with it. . . .

THE END

You give Max a cold stare, then turn away. "C'mon, Rusty," you command. Your dog stops growling and follows you.

Dennis hurries to keep up as you stride across the parking lot away from the building. Soon you're out of Max's sight.

"Whew!" sighs Dennis. "What now?"

"Let's circle around the building. Maybe we can find out what Max is up to."

"Okay," Dennis agrees hesitantly. "But let's make sure he doesn't catch us again. I don't trust him."

You lead the way around the block and down an alley. In a few minutes you have a new vantage point behind an embankment overlooking the parking lot. Max is still in the same place.

Please turn to page 115.

In a flash, you and Dennis leap up and start running toward Max's car. Since you're off to his side and behind him, Max doesn't see you. The three men by the truck are still examining the flat tires. When you're more than halfway to Max's car, one of them spots you and yells something.

"Ignore 'em, Terry!" Dennis shouts as he runs. "Get to the car!"

As you reach Max's car and Dennis jumps into the driver's seat, you see Max and one of the other men round the corner of the building, running toward you.

Dennis takes a quick look around the inside of the car. "Hey, the keys are in here!" he shouts excitedly.

"Just hurry up!" you urge him.

Dennis turns the key and moves the gearshift. The car starts to move forward.

"All right!" Dennis exclaims as the car starts to pick up speed. You help Dennis out of the car as it gains speed and starts down the grassy slope.

"Hey, you kids! What're you doing!" Max snarls. He runs toward you, pulling something from his coat pocket. It's a gun!

Dennis sees it and shouts, "Terry, get to the river!" You turn and run, feeling fear like you've never felt before. You crouch low, using the car for cover as it rolls down the slope and over the bank.

There's a big splash as Max's car hits the water, but you don't have any time to watch as you scramble along the edge of the river, trying to get away.

"Hold it, kid!" a voice snarls at you. You freeze in place for a moment, not knowing what to expect. When you turn, you see Max above you on the embankment, his gun aimed right at you. Is this the end?

Just then a mass of golden fury rushes toward Max. Max swings his gun around as Rusty leaps. The golden blur hits him just as his gun goes off. Has Rusty been hit?

Ignoring a second man running toward you with his gun drawn, you head up the embankment. You've got to see if your dog's all right!

"Wait, Terry! Look!" Dennis points to the bridge, where a pair of speeding police cars are crossing the river. The man sees them also, and he turns and starts to run.

As the police cars roar into the lot, you top the bank to see Max wrestling with Rusty. You've never seen your dog so ferocious! The pistol lies on the ground near Max, and you kick it away just as the first patrol car comes to a screeching halt beside you. Two policemen get out, with guns drawn.

"Get your dog off me, kid! Please!" Max begs.

"Rusty! Off!" you shout, and the dog releases his grip on Max's arm. Max rolls over on the ground, and one of the policemen grabs his other arm. In minutes handcuffs are on Max and the other men.

What follows is a dizzying time as you and Dennis tell the whole story. The police find Bob Gladding, Ed Segal, and Milt Davis locked inside a storage room.

It turns out that the shot from Max's pistol missed Rusty. You realize that your dog probably saved your life!

The next day, you and Dennis and Rusty are heroes. Your picture is on the front page of the local newspaper. The story says that Max was working with secret agents to steal robot technology for a foreign government.

The biggest surprise of all comes two weeks later, after you're back home. You receive a letter from the President of the United States! It reads:

Dear Terry,

The head of our country's intelligence agency has given me copies of the newspaper stories outlining your role in the recent capture of foreign agents attempting to steal important American technology. He has also given me a report on the importance of what you and your friend did to prevent this. I wish to commend you for your bravery and salute you for acting to protect our national interests.

Sincerely,
The President

It's a letter you'll always be proud of!

THE END

The truck ride isn't very long, but it seems to last forever. Where are they taking you? What's going to happen?

Finally the truck stops and the door opens. The men pull you out, and you can see that you're in another warehouse. Video arcade games are stored all around.

The men lead you through the warehouse and up several flights of stairs. You walk through an office and into a room with a single window. To your relief, one of the men removes the ropes and gags. He says nothing, but you can hear him make little grunts as he unties you. When he's finished, he looks at you coldly and leaves the room, locking the door behind him.

Please turn to page 86.

You edge your way back to Dennis to tell him about what you've seen.

"There's a guy in there with the blueprints, and I think he's going to steal them!"

"What should we do?"

"Get your bottle out! We'll sneak up to the door and you can throw it in. Then I'll slam the door shut on him."

Dennis thinks a moment, then nods. The two of you slowly move down the hallway, trying not to make any noise. The rustling sound in the room stops, and you pause, holding your breath. Then it starts again, and you both breathe a quiet sigh of relief.

At the doorway, you turn to Dennis, who has the bottle clutched in his hand. He nods that he's ready.

With that, you grab the doorknob, pressing your body against the door to give Dennis enough room to throw. Quickly, he moves to the middle of the hall and hurls the bottle into the room with all his might.

The man turns to see what the noise is just as the bottle whizzes past him and shatters in the corner of the room. There is a loud POOF! and a pinkish cloud starts to billow up from the broken bottle. You quickly slam the door shut and hold it tightly. Dennis grabs the knob, too, just in case the knockout gas doesn't work. You both wait for a minute. There's no sound from inside the room. It worked!

Carefully you and Dennis check out the rest of the office area. All the other doors are locked. No one else seems to be around, and everything appears to be all right.

"Let's go to the assembly area," you say.

"What for?"

"To see if anyone else is around. That's where the robots are."

"Okay, let's go."

Together, you, Dennis, and Rusty leave the office area and reenter the manufacturing part of the building. You crouch down behind the machines and boxes as you move. After a short time, Dennis grabs your arm.

"Listen, Terry!"

You stop for a moment. Sure enough, you hear voices speaking in a foreign language. You peer over a machine to get a look.

"Look there, Dennis." You point across the room. "See the open door? That's the research lab. They're in with the robots!"

Dennis nods. "Now what?" he asks.

"Let's get a little closer."

You creep cautiously past different kinds of machines, trying to get closer to get a better look at the men talking inside. You take up a position next to a break in the assembly line where you can see through the doorway into the research lab, but they can't see you.

There are two men inside the lab. From time to time, they talk into a walkie-talkie, and you can hear Max reply. All three robots—Bert, Gert, and Bruno—stand nearby.

"What's going on, Terry?"

"I think Max is telling them where to look."

Your hunch proves right when you see the men search through some drawers.

"What should we do?"

"I don't know. Let me think. . . ."

You chuckle to yourself. Those men are after the robots. Maybe you can turn the robots against them! You've got Bert's control panel in your pocket.

"Terry," Dennis whispers, "what about trying some of this stuff?" He holds up what looks like two tubes of toothpaste.

"What are they?"

"I found them over here. They're called Super Fast Adhesive. Listen," he says as he starts to read the label. "'Guaranteed to permanently bond metal, rubber, wood, and plastic surfaces instantly. Caution: this product hardens extremely fast.'"

"What do you want to do with it?"

"We could sneak up and put some around the doorways and then slam the doors shut. It would trap those guys inside."

1) If you want to try Dennis's idea and use the glue, turn to page 120.

2) If you want to try to activate Bert and use him against the two men, turn to page 25.

You walk over to a door with a sign that reads "SECURITY STORAGE. AUTHORIZED PERSONNEL ONLY." You turn the handle, but the door is locked tight. Then you hear a muffled noise from beyond the door, like a thumping sound.

Dennis hears it, too. "What's that sound?" he asks.

"I don't know." You listen as the thumping continues, first slow, then fast, then slow again.

On a hunch, you tap on the door. The noise stops, but to your surprise, someone taps back from inside!

"It's Morse code!" you exclaim excitedly, finally recognizing the unusual pattern of the taps.

Dennis starts to ask something, but you motion to him to be quiet so you can listen. Even Rusty cocks an ear.

The taps are repeated. You listen carefully, thinking back to when you made your own telegraph set and learned Morse code.

"H-E-L-P," you say slowly as you hear the letters tapped out. "Somebody's calling for help!"

You grab the doorknob again and try to wrench the door open. You shake the handle, but it's locked and won't budge. You tap back your own message: "T-H-I-S I-S T-E-R-R-Y. W-H-O A-R-E Y-O-U?"

It takes time, but an answer comes back: "B-O-B, E-D, M-I-L-T. T-I-E-D U-P. T-H-R-E-E

M-E-N W-A-N-T R-O-B-O-T P-L-A-N-S. G-E-T
H-E-L-P."

1) If you want to leave the building and
   call the police, turn to page 99.

2) If you want to try to break the door
   down to rescue Bob, Milt, and Ed, turn
   to page 131.

3) If you want to go to the manufacturing
   area to look for the three men, then
   come back later to help Bob, Ed, and
   Milt, turn to page 141.

4) If you want to go to the office area to
   look for the three men, then come back
   later to help Bob, Ed, and Milt, turn to
   page 16.

Slowly you extend your hand to give Max the controller unit. You don't want Dennis or Rusty to get hurt.

Max smiles, then snatches the controller from your hand. "You're dumber than I thought! Now, get over there, both of you!"

He shoves you and Dennis into a corner as Rusty starts to growl again.

"Shut up, mutt!" Max snarls. But Rusty steps toward him slowly, still growling.

"Stupid mutt!" Max yells. "You asked for it!" He twists a dial and pushes a button on the controller. Bert turns to face Rusty, and the Taser dart shoots through the air. Rusty collapses to the floor, motionless.

"My dog! You've killed my dog!" All thoughts of your own safety gone, you lunge toward Max just as he retracts the Taser device back into the front of the robot's body. The big man knocks you to the floor.

"Stay back, kid. You know what this thing can do. You wanna be next?"

You know full well that Max would use the Taser device on you. Feeling helpless, you gaze at Rusty. Is your dog dead?

"We'd better do as he says," Dennis urges.

"Smart kid." Max raises the walkie-talkie to his mouth and speaks in a strange language. Soon, another man arrives and they speak the same language. Suddenly you find yourself being tied and gagged. As you are led away, you turn your head and see Rusty, lying still on the floor.

The men lead you inside the truck and make you sit. Then, one by one, they wheel the robots, Bert, Gert, and Bruno, inside with you. Then they pull down the sliding door at the rear of the truck, and a loud click tells you it's locked. Darkness surrounds you, and as the truck starts moving, you realize you're trapped!

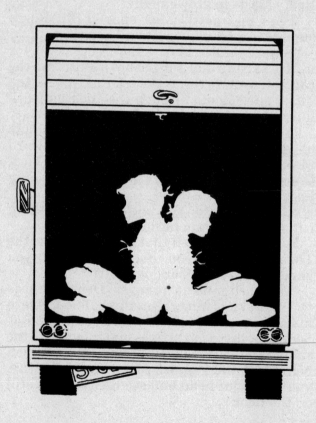

Even though your hands are tied behind you, you and Dennis try to untie each other. But the truck bounces around and your hands are too tightly bound to use them much. Finally you both give up, exhausted.

After a ride of about ten minutes, the door opens. Max and three other men drag you out and guide you through an old warehouse containing row upon row of video games. Normally Dennis would be in heaven here, but instead you see only fear in his eyes.

The two of you are taken up several flights of stairs, through an office, and into a room with a single window. Max unties your hands and arms, then removes the gag from your mouth. You stare at him coldly, but he just laughs as he starts for the door.

"Enjoy your stay, kids!" With that, he closes the door and locks you in the room with Dennis.

Please turn to page 86.

You edge your way back to Dennis and describe your plan in a soft whisper.

"Are you crazy?" Dennis protests. "How can we jump him?"

"We've just gotta surprise him, that's all! We'll sneak up next to the door, then I'll give a signal and we'll rush in and tackle him."

"Do you really think your plan will work, Terry?" Dennis asks.

"Sure it will. They do it all the time on TV. Let's go!" Without waiting for Dennis to have more doubts, you turn and tiptoe down the corridor. Dennis and Rusty follow silently.

Again you pause at the doorway, tipping your head slightly to see if the large man has moved. His back is still toward you. You're sure your plan will work!

You look back at Dennis and see fear on his face, but you also see him steel himself. He takes a deep breath, looks you in the eye, and nods. This is it!

You tense your body and signal Dennis. But just as you start to dash into the room, Rusty growls loudly.

It's too late to stop! You burst through the doorway as fast as you can, with Dennis right behind you. But the man has heard Rusty and turns around. You can't surprise him anymore, but you can't stop, either. You leap toward the big man, hoping to tackle him to the floor. But in spite of his size, he's quick. He dodges you, and you end up tackling the table instead of him.

Dennis has little better luck, and the big man shrugs him off easily. Now he's shouting into his walkie-talkie in some kind of foreign accent.

"Max? Boris. Is big trouble here! Two kids and dog in room! Quickly, come!"

You've got to stop him! You get up and throw yourself at him again. But it's no use. He's just too big and too strong. He seems to flick you away like a fly. Rusty barks and growls and makes one or two lunges at him, but Rusty is a pet, not a fighter.

Now the man is coming toward you! You're cornered! A big hand reaches out for you and grabs you on the shoulder. You kick and swing at him, but your blows don't seem to have any effect. Another big hand clamps over your mouth like a vise, and then everything goes black.

When you come to your senses, you find yourself in the back of the truck. Dennis is beside you and, like you, bound and gagged. Heavy crates surround you. You hear the sound of the engine starting, and you're on your way . . . but to where?

Please turn to page 37.

You look the two men directly in the eyes. "Who are you?" you demand.

Instead of replying, the men grab you and Dennis and pull you inside the door. Rusty starts to bark loudly, but the door slams, shutting him outside.

The men push you to the floor and tie you up. You try to fight them, but they're too strong for you. You watch helplessly as Dennis is tied up, too. Then a rag is stuffed into your mouth. As you wonder what's going to happen, fear grows inside you uncontrollably.

You hear the men talking in some foreign language. Then Max's voice comes over the radio, but he, too, speaks the strange language, offering no hint of your fate. The men carry you through the building and then lay you down in the back of the truck. Dennis is placed alongside you. You both struggle to get free, but the ropes hold you too tightly.

Soon you see the men sliding some large packing crates along the floor. What's going on?

In a few minutes, the truck doors are slammed shut and the motor starts up, sending a cold chill up your spine.

The truck starts to move, and you're on your way to somewhere. But where?

Please turn to page 37.

You can tell that Dennis is glad when you agree to try his idea. You're pretty sure he was scared to hide in the truck. After a look around, you lower yourselves down from the loading dock. Rusty jumps down after you.

"Let's do the rear tires," Dennis suggests.

"Okay, but be careful, and keep listening, in case anyone comes."

Dennis crouches down by one rear wheel of the truck, while you go around to the other side. You look to make sure Max is out of sight. No one is around, so you grab the tire valve and push the center in with your thumbnail. The air begins to escape with a loud hiss. You desperately hope that no one hears it.

You watch as the tire starts to lose its shape. It seems to take hours, but finally the rim touches the pavement.

"Did you get yours?" Dennis asks.

"Yeah, it's real flat!"

"These guys aren't going anywhere!" Dennis laughs at the thought of the men trying to drive off with flat tires.

"Let's go!"

"Where?"

"Up on the bridge. We can use the phone there to call the cops."

You sneak away from the truck by crouching down and moving carefully, keeping the landscaped embankments between you and Max. Rusty scampers along behind.

Once you're up on the bridge, you have a good vantage point to watch Max again.

Dennis uses the phone to call the 911 emergency number and tells the police dispatcher what's happened. He breathes a sigh of relief as he hangs up the telephone.

"The cops will be here in a couple of minutes," he tells you.

"Good. We can't let these guys get away with this!" You remember all the work you put in on Bert and how attached you are to him, even if he is just a robot. But then Dennis brings you back to the present.

"Terry, they still have Max's car to use to make a getaway."

"Not if the cops get here right away."

"What if they don't? We've got to stop them!"

"How?"

"See how Max's car is parked? If he leaves it, we can run down there and put it in neutral and it'll roll downhill—right out of the parking lot, across the grass, and into the river!"

"You think that'll work?"

"Sure! See how steep the parking lot is there?"

Before you can think about it, you see the two men come out of the building at the loading dock. One of them is ready to get into the cab of the truck when he notices the flat tires. He shouts to the other man, and the two of them examine the tires.

A third man—one you haven't seen before—comes out of the building. In a second, they're calling Max on their walkie-talkie. One man

MORTON ELECTRONICS

pulls a gun from his coat and starts looking around the other side of the truck.

Max leaves his car and sets out at a run across the parking lot toward the truck.

Dennis grabs your arm. "Now, Terry! This is our chance!"

1) If you want to try Dennis's plan to roll Max's car into the river, turn to page 33.

2) If you want to stay where you are and wait for the police to arrive, turn to page 109.

You run over to Dennis and grab him. "You're going the wrong way! This isn't the way out!"

"But, Terry, I—"

You don't give him a chance to finish, because Bruno is almost upon you. Max snickers as he follows his sinister black robot.

"C'mon!" You pull Dennis toward the warehouse door. Rusty runs ahead of you, as if he knows the way out, too.

As you approach the exit, you can hear Max talking into his radio and laughing. You turn the corner around an assembly line and find out why. The door is closed!

You run up to the door and try to pull it open, but it won't budge. Then you hear Max's booming voice. "It's locked, and I've got the key. You're not getting out of here!"

You look around for a way to escape, but Bruno and Max have you cornered. The robot's claw arm reaches out toward you, its sharp fingers clicking open and shut.

"Don't try anything," Max commands, "or this robot'll give you the shock of your lives! Its Taser dart has a lot more juice than yours." You know he's right, so you stay put.

In a minute another man joins Max. "Tie 'em up!" Max barks. "And take care of the dog so he doesn't bother us."

Rusty gives a low growl as the man grabs a large cardboard box and turns it upside down. As you move to stop him, Max shouts, "Hold it, kid! One more step and you're gonna wish you hadn't!" He glares at you and nervously fingers the robot controller in his hand.

The other man takes the box and puts it over Rusty, then places a heavy metal robot part he finds nearby on top of it. Rusty whines and scratches the box, but it's no use—he's trapped inside.

Next the man finds some heavy twine and ties up you and Dennis. Your hands and arms are bound behind you, and a gag is placed in your mouth.

"Get them into the truck," Max says as he unlocks the door. The man shoves you and Dennis ahead of him into the warehouse. As you walk you can hear Rusty, still scratching and whining under the box.

The man puts you and Dennis in the back of the truck and locks it. Your eyes aren't used to the darkness yet, but you hear Dennis beside you, probably just as scared as you are. Max and the man return a few minutes later with two other men. They open the door and wheel the robots into the back of the truck beside you. Then the door is slammed shut once more, and darkness surrounds you again.

Please turn to page 37.

· You pick out a good spot to hide among some large boxes. A couple of them are lower than the others, so that you and Dennis can stand on them and have a view of the whole warehouse. You wait in silence for something to happen.

THUMP, THUMP, THUMP, THUMP!

The sound seems to be coming from right behind you! You turn expectantly, your heart pounding wildly.

It's only Rusty, wagging his tail against a box! "Whew!" Both you and Dennis breathe a sigh of relief and almost laugh at the thought of being scared by your dog. You quiet Rusty down and continue your lookout.

After a while, it becomes apparent that nothing is happening in the warehouse.

"What now?" Dennis whispers.

You think about the possibilities. There are two other places in the building to check.

"We can check out either the manufacturing area or the offices. C'mon!"

1) If you want to go to the manufacturing area, where the research lab with the robots is located, turn to page 141.

2) If you want to check out the office area, where the blueprint room and your uncle's office are, turn to page 16.

You run through the warehouse first, calling out, "Ed! Milt! Bob!" But there is no answer.

Next you head for the manufacturing area, where assembly lines fill the large, open room. You call again, but again no one answers. You glance into the research lab, but no one is there, either. Where is everyone?

You haven't checked the offices yet, so you head that way, opening doors and calling out, "Ed! Milt! Bob!" Still no answer.

"Dennis, something's got to be wrong! Let's call the police." But when you try to use a wall phone in the hallway, the line is dead. "It doesn't work!" you tell Dennis, almost in a panic.

"Let's get out of here, Terry!" says Dennis, sounding scared.

"Okay. This way."

You, Dennis, and Rusty turn around to head back out of the building. But no sooner do you reach the manufacturing area than you see Max!

You pull Dennis into a hiding place, with questions tumbling in your mind. Why did Max leave the parking lot? Did he hear you calling Milt and Ed? Did he see you? You and Dennis watch silently as Max approaches. Maybe he won't see you.

But Rusty knows Max is the enemy and begins to growl. You peek out from your hiding place, and there's Max, looking straight at you, his face red with anger. He looks from you to the small box in his hand. You see him press buttons and turn a dial. Then you hear clicking and whirring sounds.

"What's that?" Dennis asks, puzzled.

You know very well what it is, and your fear deepens. "It's a robot!" you shout. "He's sending a robot after us!"

The clicking and whirring become louder, and Max's robot, Bruno, comes into view. Its shiny black body rumbles along on fat rubber tires. Its menacing claw arm swings from side to side. Even though it's rapidly approaching you, Dennis seems more interested in it than afraid of it.

"C'mon!" you shout. "This way!" You and Rusty start toward the door to the warehouse.

Dennis suddenly realizes he's in danger where he is, and he starts to move—but in a different direction. He goes toward a corner of the manufacturing area where there are high stacks of cartons. "Over here, Terry. I've got an idea!"

Why is Dennis going another way? Should you go with him or make him come back your way? You've got to decide quickly, because Max's robot is coming fast!

1) If you want to grab Dennis and take him toward the door, turn to page 55.

2) If you want to follow Dennis, turn to page 135.

You and Dennis crouch down to watch the two men in the research lab. Rusty waits patiently beside you. The two men continue their search, occasionally talking on the radio with Max as they gather papers and electronic parts. Max is helping them to steal everything!

After a short time, they turn their attention to the three robots, Bert, Gert, and Bruno.

"What are they doing, Terry?" asks Dennis.

"I don't know, but I hope they don't hurt the robots!"

The men move around behind Bert and Gert, then open a panel on each robot. Fear grips you.

"Oh, no!" you gasp as you watch the men remove something from each robot.

"What is it?" Dennis asks.

"It's the power pack! That's what makes them run!"

You watch in stunned silence as the men start to take the robots apart. All your summer's work is being undone! You want to stop them, but you know you can't. When they disconnect Bert's arm, it feels almost like losing your own.

"They're putting them in boxes, Terry!" You can hardly watch as the men pack the robots into three big boxes, just like the ones you saw in the back of the rental truck.

"They're going to get away with them!" you whisper. "We've got to stop them!"

"What should we do?"

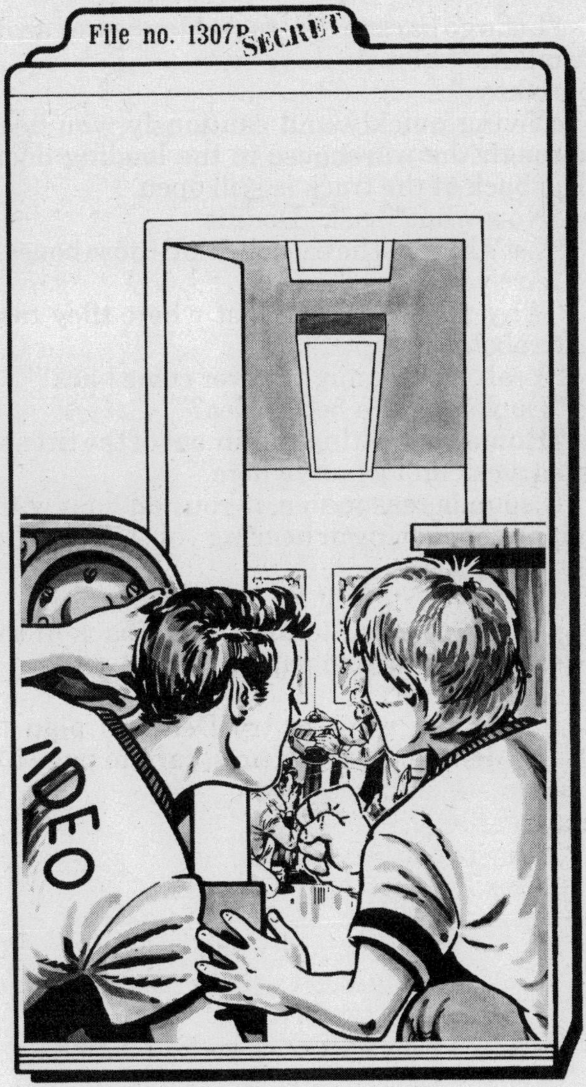

File no. 1307B
SECRET

"Let's go back to the truck. Maybe we can do something to it."

"Okay."

Moving quickly and cautiously, you head through the warehouse to the loading dock. The back of the truck is still open.

"Now what?" asks Dennis.

"Let's hide in the truck behind those boxes."

"Are you crazy?"

"Why not? We'll find out where they take the robots."

"Yeah, but we might never come back!"

"Do you have a better idea?"

"How about letting the air out of the tires so the truck can't go anywhere?"

It sounds reasonable, if you can do it without anyone seeing or hearing you. Now you've got to decide. . . .

1) If you want to hide in the back of the truck, turn to page 65.

2) If you want to try Dennis's plan to deflate the truck tires, turn to page 51.

You and Dennis discuss his plan under cover of the noises from the Robot Escape game.

"First we get them to open the door," Dennis explains. "We'll say we've got to go to the bathroom. Once we're out the door, we'll make a break for it!"

"It sounds too simple, but let's try it. I'll try anything to get out of here!"

Dennis goes over to the door and pounds on it to get someone's attention. In a few seconds Max opens it. "Whattaya want?" he snarls.

"We need to use the bathroom."

"It's over there." He points across the office.

You and Dennis step through the door. "Now!" he shouts. You both make a break for the stairway.

Behind you, you hear Max yell, "Hey! Get those kids!"

Stride for stride, the two of you race across the room and start down the stairs. You don't dare take time to look back, but you can hear them coming behind you. It sounds like they're gaining on you!

"Keep going!" Dennis shouts at the landing one flight below. You continue down to what looks like the ground floor. But you can't tell which way is out! There's no time to waste, so you turn left and start running between piles of plywood. You hear the men charging after you.

"Now we've got 'em!" you hear Max shout. And as you find yourselves in a dead end, you

know he's right. You try to climb over the
stacks of wood, but one of the men grabs you.
In a moment Max is facing you.

"I told you kids not to try anything, but you
wouldn't listen! Well, this time you've been too
smart for your own good. You've just earned
yourselves a one-way plane ride with your
robot friends. Too bad you didn't bring a
coat—it gets awfully cold at forty thousand
feet in the belly of a cargo jet.

"Tie 'em up!" With that, two of the men grab
you and take you back upstairs. You struggle
to get free, but it's no use.

Please turn to page 20.

"C'mon!" you whisper to Dennis as you make your way into the back of the truck.

"Wait! Rusty doesn't want to go!"

Sure enough, your dog is pacing around the loading dock and refuses to enter the truck with you. Even when you call him, he refuses to come and whines instead.

"Quiet him down, Terry!" Dennis cautions.

You hurry to Rusty and try to pick him up, but he squirms and whines so much that you know it won't work. You crouch down to calm him.

"Go home, boy! Home to Uncle Sid's!"

At first Rusty won't go, but finally he looks at you one last time and jumps off the loading dock and starts to head for home.

There's no time to waste, so you and Dennis hurry into the truck and hide among the large boxes. You've just taken your places when you hear footsteps and voices of at least two men. They're speaking Russian! You hear heavy objects being wheeled into the truck. The men come so close that you have to hold your breath to make sure they don't hear you.

Finally you hear them leave the truck, but then your heart jumps into your throat as they close the rear door. A click tells you you're locked in! It's pitch black inside, and you and Dennis are alone, going to . . . where?

"Terry?"

"Yeah?"

"I don't think this was such a hot idea."

"Yeah, I know. . . ." You begin to think that

maybe Dennis was right, especially when you realize you don't have any idea of where you're going, how far away it might be, and what's going to happen when you get there.

You hear the men talking some more outside, and then they get into the cab of the truck. The doors slam shut and the engine starts with a roar. In a minute you're moving.

What if you're on your way to Los Angeles? Or New York? You could be in here forever! You're wondering how long it will take for Uncle Sid to miss you when suddenly the truck stops and then backs up. It's only been a few minutes, so maybe it's not going to be such a long trip, after all.

You close your eyes against the sudden glare as the rear door slides open and the men start to unload the boxes. You and Dennis stay as still as possible. Your heart is pounding as box after box is carried off. You're still hidden when the men stand outside the truck and talk some more.

Maybe they won't find you! But then the talking stops, and two men return to the truck and start taking more boxes. There's nowhere to move to as the last box is removed.

You see the surprise in the men's faces when Dennis shouts, "Run for it!" He tries to get past the men, and you spring up to follow. But it's no use—there just isn't room enough to get by them. They may be surprised, but they react fast enough to grab both of you. They search you and take away your robot controller and Dennis's bottle of knockout gas.

One man sticks his head out the rear door and shouts something. In a moment, Max is there, glowering at you.

"Stupid kids!" he barks. "You can't keep out of trouble, can you?" He bends down and puts his face right up to yours. "Well, you've got plenty of trouble now!" You can see the hatred in Max's beady little eyes, and you feel the contempt in his voice.

"And there's no Bob Gladding or Uncle Sidney to help you this time!" Max glares at you for a moment, then backs away. "Lock 'em up!" he snaps to the men. They pull you and Dennis away roughly.

The men march you through an old warehouse filled with different kinds of video games. You're taken up several flights of stairs, through an office, and into a small room with a single window. The men leave the room, and you hear the sound of a key turning in the lock.

Please turn to page 86.

"The bottle!" you shout to Dennis. "Throw the bottle!"

Dennis doesn't even hesitate. He just grabs the bottle from his pocket and smashes it in the doorway, right at the feet of the two men. You both back away as a cloud of pink gas rises in front of them. They look surprised for just a moment, then collapse to the floor. It worked!

"Hey, you kids!" booms Max from behind you. Turning, you see him start to leave his car to come after you.

"C'mon, Dennis! Let's go!" you shout as you take off at a run, with Rusty at your heels, toward the warehouse end of the plant. At the far end of the building, you turn the corner and see an angry Max sprinting across the parking lot after you. Suddenly those gym classes you've never liked very much seem worthwhile!

"This way!" you shout to Dennis as you head for the loading dock, where the rental truck is parked. As you approach, you can see that the loading dock door is open. There is a gap between the end of the truck and the edge of the doorway. It looks big enough to squeeze through.

Quickly you pull yourself up through the gap, with Dennis right behind you. "Up, Rusty!" you call as the dog hesitates. He seems to sense your fear as you look back at Max. Rusty crouches and springs up onto the dock just in time! Max rounds the corner of the

building and heads toward the loading dock.
Now you've got to do some fast thinking.

1) If you decide to go through the plant
   and try to find the guards to help you,
   go to page 58.

2) If you decide to go to the research lab
   and try to activate your robot to use
   against Max, turn to page 96.

Dennis starts to back up, but you hold your ground as Max advances toward you. You've never seen anyone so angry before. If you're going to fool him, it's going to have to be pretty convincing!

Max starts to say something, but you cut him off. "The game's over, Max. You're finished!" Your boldness takes him by surprise, and Dennis looks at you with awe. Max stops in his tracks, and you continue the bluff.

"The police are on their way. You're all washed up, Max."

Max stares at you. "It's not possible, kid. All the phones are dead!"

"Sorry, Max, but we called the cops before we came in here. They'll be here any minute. You'd better get out of here while you can."

Max looks puzzled and uncertain. You can tell he's not sure if you're bluffing him or not. Finally he starts to back up toward the door.

"All right, kid, but you're gonna pay for this later!" he warns as he turns and bolts for the door. Once he's gone, you and Dennis each breathe a sigh of relief.

"That took a lot of guts, Terry!" Dennis says. "I didn't think he was going believe you!"

"I was worried, too," you admit. "I don't know what would've happened if he hadn't believed me!" An empty feeling in your stomach reminds you of how close a call it was. . . .

"Now let's call the cops," Dennis suggests. The two of you leave the building just as Max drives off, abandoning his partners altogether.

You use the phone on the bridge to call the police, and they arrive in just a few minutes.

With the police, you go back into the plant, and they capture all three of the agents. They also find Bob Gladding, Ed Segal, and Milt Davis tied up in a storage room and set them free.

Detectives arrive and question you and Dennis about what happened. Then two more men show up. They say they work for the government but won't tell you any more than that. They ask all about the robots and about Max.

After you get back to your uncle's house, some newspaper reporters come to interview you. They take your picture with Rusty, and the next day it appears next to a picture of Dennis in the paper. There's also a story about how Max was caught by the police when he tried to board a plane for Tokyo.

Your Uncle Sid throws a big party for you and Dennis before you leave for home. It's a perfect ending after all the excitement at the plant.

A few weeks after you get home, it looks like the whole thing is forgotten, but then one Saturday when you're home alone, a woman calls on the phone.

"Is this the Terry Morton who was involved with the robots at the Morton Electronics plant?" she asks. When you tell her it is, she says, "I've got something special for you, and

I'd like you to meet me downtown behind the courthouse in half an hour."

You're puzzled. "How will I know you?" you ask.

"Don't worry. I know what you look like. Just be there." Before you can say more, she hangs up.

It's all very mysterious. Should you go down to the courthouse to find out what this is all about—and maybe start a new adventure? Or should you just stay home and not worry about it? It's a tough decision. . . .

THE END

"Call the police," you tell Dennis. "Rusty and I will stay here to guard Max."

"Okay, but I'll have to go up on the bridge if none of the phones here work."

"Okay, but hurry!"

Dennis runs off while you keep an eye on Max. He moves slightly from time to time, but you can tell he's still unconscious. Somehow, you don't feel sorry for him.

It takes a long time, but Dennis finally returns. "The cops will be here any minute!" he says. "But when I was up on the bridge, I saw another guy come out of the building from the other door. He had some big rolls of paper under his arm."

"Where'd he go?"

"He got into Max's car and drove away. What do you think he took?"

"It must have been the blueprints of the robots!"

You wait impatiently for the police, knowing that every minute the blueprints are getting farther away.

Soon you hear sirens, and a few moments later the police swarm all over the building. They grab Max and put handcuffs on him. They search the building and find Bob Gladding, Ed Segal, and Milt Davis tied up and locked inside the storage room.

After Max and the other men are taken away, some detectives arrive to question you and Dennis. One of the detectives identifies herself as an FBI agent. She explains that

Max was working with foreign agents to steal robot technology from the Morton plant. She praises you for stopping them and says that you've helped the FBI greatly.

The next day you and Dennis are surprised to see your pictures in the paper, along with a story about the spy ring's capture. The story calls you both heroes!

A few months later, you visit Dennis and your uncle when you come back to testify at Max's trial. You hate to see anyone go to prison for twenty years, but Max deserves it if anyone does!

The day before you're scheduled to fly home, Dennis comes to your uncle's house. He takes you aside and says secretly, "You know that guy who escaped with the blueprints? I've got an idea of how to track him down and get the blueprints back, but it's risky." As you see the intense look on Dennis's face and remember other ideas he's had, you know you want to hear his plan. . . .

THE END

"I'm going to use Bert to stop those guys," you whisper to Dennis as you pull the controller unit from your pocket.

"Are you sure it will work?"

"Sure. Are you ready?"

Dennis nods and strains to see your robot in action. You press a button and Bert comes to life.

The men in the room look up in surprise. With arms raised, Bert advances toward one of the men. The agent backs away, but Bert grabs him firmly with his steel arms.

The other spy rushes over and starts to hit Bert with a piece of metal he grabs from the lab bench. CLANG! CLANG! Bert is tough, but you've got to do something before they damage him!

"Let them have it with the Taser dart, Terry!" Dennis urges.

"Okay! Here goes!"

There's a short buzz as the dart shoots out of Bert's body and into the man in his grasp. The agent goes limp, and Bert lets him drop to the floor. The Taser device retracts into Bert's body, and he turns toward the second man.

But the other spy has seen enough. He runs out the lab door, shouting into his hand-held radio.

"C'mon, Dennis!" you say. "We've got to make sure Bert is okay."

Inside the lab, Dennis looks down at the limp form on the floor. "Is he dead?"

"No. He'll wake up in a little while and be

okay. There's only enough juice to stun some-one. Hey, look at this!" you say angrily, point-ing at Bert's metallic body. "They dented him!"

You check Bert carefully to see if they've damaged him anywhere else. There are some scratches and a couple of small dents, but he seems all right.

At that moment, Max bursts into the room, his beady eyes red with anger. "You kids are in for it now!" he says with a sneer. He reaches out and grabs the controller for his robot from the counter. He presses a button and Bruno starts up. It's going to be a robot fight!

Max's face twists into an evil grin. "I'll show you what a REAL robot can do!"

"That's what YOU think, Max! That pile of junk of yours is no match for Bert!" You've waited all summer to tell him off!

"That's big talk, kid! Your puny little thing doesn't stand a chance against a machine thirty pounds heavier!"

Max maneuvers Bruno around to face Bert, and you see the light glint off its shiny black body, its huge menacing claw arm upraised.

There's not a moment to waste! You extend Bert's arms and advance him toward Bruno. Suddenly there's a blinding flash from the black robot's spotlight. Stunned for a moment, you close your eyes to protect them from the overpowering beam of light.

"Get the light, Terry!" Dennis shouts.

You squint your eyes to see where the light's

coming from so that you can send Bert after it. Both his arms reach out for the spotlight. There's a big POP! and the light goes out.

Dennis starts to pick things up from the tables in the lab and throw them at Bruno. As the black robot's claw arm closes into a giant, threatening fist, Dennis heaves a chunk of metal at the mechanical monster. It bounces off harmlessly.

"Forget Bruno, Dennis. Get Max!" you shout. "Rusty! Get him!" Snarling, the dog lunges toward the big man.

Bruno's giant fist lashes out at Bert and lands with a sickening clang. Bert shakes from the force of the blow, but he seems all right. He turns on his clicking treads and raises his arms. If you can grab Bruno's claw arm, maybe you can stop him!

"One more blow like that and your precious robot'll be a pile of junk, kid!" Max yells. His words turn into a howl of pain as Rusty clamps his jaws into Max's leg. Now's your chance!

Bert's arms reach up and grab Bruno's claw arm. You tighten Bert's grip and hold on.

"Oh, no, you don't, kid!" Max frantically presses buttons on his controller, but his robot can't force its way out of Bert's vicelike grip.

Bruno's claw clicks open and closed, but it's harmless in Bert's grasp. You've got him now, if you can only tip him over! Bert surges forward, his tracks churning powerfully. Just a little bit more. . . .

With a thunderous crash, the big black machine topples to the floor, its wheels spinning harmlessly.

Max curses loudly, then throws down his hand controller and starts to reach under his coat.

"Watch out, Terry!" shouts Dennis. "He might have a gun!"

In a flash, Bert turns on Max. You see a glint of black steel in Max's hand. It IS a gun!

Without hesitating, you press the Taser button, and the dart shoots out and into Max's leg. There's a buzz and Max's whole body recoils from the shock. He freezes in place and then drops in a heap as the gun falls harmlessly to the floor.

"Nice going, Terry! You got him! You got him!" Dennis eagerly slaps you on the back in congratulation.

You reach down and pick up Max's gun. It's heavier than the pistols you learned how to use at summer camp, and it looks much more powerful. It's a good thing Max didn't get a chance to use it!

"Behind you, Terry!" Dennis shouts.

Without thinking, you swing around and point the gun at another man who is running into the lab. He stops abruptly, throws up his hands, and starts jabbering in a foreign language.

"I think he wants to surrender," Dennis says. It's hard to tell what he's saying, but it looks as though Dennis is right . . . especially when the man slowly removes a gun from his coat and gingerly sets it down.

Dennis runs to call the police while you keep the man guarded. It takes a while, but eventually he returns with a bunch of police officers.

Max is just starting to stir again when they slap the handcuffs on him and take him away. The other man just seems relieved that it's over. After everything that's happened, you kind of feel that way, too.

When the chief detective and a man from the FBI arrive, they both seem impressed by what you and Dennis have done. After they finish questioning the two of you, the FBI man says that he wants to recommend you for a presidential citation. It sounds like a nice idea, but you don't give it too much thought. When your photo appears in the newspaper the next day, that's thrill enough.

A few weeks later, you get a special letter from the White House. It's from the President himself! You tear open the envelope and read it eagerly:

Dear Terry,

I have received a full report of your actions in protecting the valuable work of the Morton Electronics Company from foreign espionage activities. Your quick thinking and bravery exemplify exactly what our country needs to protect itself from foreign agents bent upon stealing our national secrets and technology. Accordingly, I am pleased to award you the

President's Medal in honor of your actions. I wish to thank you on behalf of all Americans.

In addition, should you decide in the future that you wish to enroll in one of the U.S. Service Academies—Army, Navy, Air Force, Coast Guard, or Merchant Marine—please contact me. If you meet certain minimum qualifications, I will exert the influence of my office to see that you receive a congressional appointment.

The President

First your picture in the paper, and now this! You can hardly believe it's really happening, but there's the letter, right in your hand. You can imagine what the kids at school will say when they hear about this!

THE END

You and Dennis pass the time by playing the two Robot Escape games and trying to see who can run up the highest score. It helps keep your mind off other things. When you beat Dennis's best on your fourth game, you feel pretty good.

After an hour or so, you hear a phone ring in the office outside. Max answers it, and you can hear his booming voice.

"Max here!... Yeah, we're all ready to go.... Flight 808? Right. We'll be at the cargo gate in forty-five minutes. We had a little unexpected trouble here, but we've taken care of it. No problem. ... All right. See you at the gate." Max hangs up the phone, and you can hear the men starting to move around.

A key turns in the lock, and the door of your prison opens. Max and another man enter. "Come here, kid!" Max barks. "You and your friend are going to be here awhile, while the rest of us take a little trip. I hope the robots like their new home. Ha, ha!" Max's laugh is so evil it makes you sick. You want to tell him how much you despise him, but you don't know if you dare make him angry.

1) If you want to tell Max what you think of him, turn to page 95.

2) If you decide to keep quiet and say nothing, turn to page 118.

After a while in your new place of captivity, fear begins to release its grip on you and give way to a feeling of relief that you're still alive.

"Are you okay?" you ask Dennis.

"Yeah—just a little scared. We're lucky we're still alive!"

"I know," you reply, thinking about what you've just gone through. "Do you have any idea where this place is?"

"Somewhere on the west side of town," Dennis says, peering out the window.

"How do you know that?"

"I can see planes landing and taking off from the airport. And I can see the back of the water tower from here."

"Check the window. Can you open it?"

Dennis tugs at the window. "Nah. It's sealed shut or something. Besides, we're too high up to jump down. This must be at least the third floor."

Just then the door rattles, and you hear a key turn in the lock. Dennis scrambles away from the window, and you both try to look innocent. The door swings open and Max strides in.

"You kids enjoying your little visit?" His voice is full of contempt.

"We don't like it here," Dennis offers.

"Don't like it here, eh? What's the matter, not enough excitement for you?" he says with a sneer. "Well, I don't like it here very much, either. That's why I'm leaving, and soon, too—along with everything we took from the

Morton plant. But you kids are going to be here for a while. In fact, by the time they find you here, we'll be in Tokyo, or maybe even Vladivostok. And we'll have all the robots and the plans." Max turns to you and chuckles evilly. "How does that grab you?"

You stay silent, because you're too angry to talk straight. If anyone ever deserved to be hated, Max does.

"You kids'll be here a long time, so I'm gonna do you a real favor," Max goes on. He turns and calls into the other room, "Boris! Bring those two units in here!"

Through the open door, you see a man wheeling a cart toward the room. On it are two full-size video arcade games. Just as the man gets to the door, he bumps against the fire extinguisher mounted on the wall, and it falls to the floor with a loud crash. Max collars the man quickly.

"You clumsy oaf! Pick it up!" He pushes the man backward, then finishes wheeling the cart into the room himself. As you watch, he slides both machines off the cart and plugs them into wall outlets. Immediately they hum to life.

"I picked these two machines out just for you, Terry, since I know you like to play. They're a new game called Robot Escape. I thought you'd find the subject appropriate!" Max bellows his evil laugh.

"We're shipping the robots by air freight in a shipment of arcade games," Max goes on.

"They happen to fit right into these packing crates, and when we adjust the weights, no one will be the wiser.

"So enjoy yourself, hotshot! And one more thing—don't try anything funny. If you do try something stupid, I'll make you wish you hadn't!"

With that, he goes out the door, slams it shut, and locks it.

You and Dennis stand in stunned silence for a moment. Then Dennis steps over to one of the machines, presses the start button, and begins to play. "Might as well try out this game," he says.

Amid the buzzes and beeps from the arcade game, you sit back on a stool and look around the room, trying to figure a way out. The room looks like a repair shop for electronic arcade games. The counters are littered with transistors, diodes, circuit boards, junctions, and all kinds of parts. On the wall are coils of insulated electrical wire. Parts of games are scattered all over.

"A hundred thousand points!" Dennis shouts, momentarily interrupting your thoughts. You ignore him and concentrate on ways you might possibly escape.

There's a buzz as Dennis's game ends. "A hundred and nine thousand!" Dennis crows. "Want to try it?"

It hardly seems like a time to be playing games to you. "Nah. Help me try to figure a way out of here."

Dennis pulls up a stool and sits down next to
you. He scans the walls and looks around the
room.

"We could just try to make a break for it,"
Dennis suggests.

"Yeah, but we'd have to find the right way
out of this building on the first try."

"Well, maybe we could use that fire extinguisher on them. There might even be another
one around."

"Yeah ... that might work. But how are we
going to get out the door in the first place?"

"That's easy! We'll just tell them we've got
to go to the bathroom. They've got to let us out
for that."

You continue to look around as you talk.
Suddenly your eye fixes on the coils of wire
hanging on the wall, and another idea comes
to mind. "What about using the wire as a rope
and escaping out the window?"

"Is it strong enough—and long enough?"

"We'd have to use more than one wire to
support us, but it looks like there's plenty."

Dennis's eye is caught by something. "Terry,
what's that box on the wall over there?" He
points toward a corner.

"It's a junction box for telephone lines, I
think. It probably has all the phone lines from
the building in it." You walk over to the box
and open it. You discover that your guess was
right.

"Can we use it for anything?"

"Well, I know a little about how they work.

Maybe I could rig up something with that and the other stuff we've got in here."

Dennis seems to have second thoughts, however. "I don't know, Terry. Maybe we should just do what Max says. I think he really meant it when he said we'd better not try anything."

1) If you decide you want to get Max to open the door and then make a run for it, turn to page 63.

2) If you want to try to grab fire extinguishers and fight Max and the other men with them, turn to page 154.

3) If you want to use the electrical wire as a rope and try to escape through the window, turn to page 103.

4) If you want to try to hook into the telephone lines and send a message for help, turn to page 124.

5) If you want to follow Max's warning and just stay where you are, turn to page 85.

You decide that it's best not to mess around with Max in the ugly mood he's in. As long as Uncle Sid knew Max was going to be around, it's probably all right.

Instead, you and Dennis try out the bottle of knockout gas down by the river. Dennis is pleased when you actually put a couple of muskrats to sleep for a short time. They awaken unharmed.

Taking the long way home, you stop at the shopping mall and find out that there is a new game at the arcade. You feel pretty good when you beat Dennis on the third try.

When you get home, you wait for Bob Gladding's call, but it doesn't come. When you call the plant, there's no answer either. Then at six o'clock, just as your Uncle Sid arrives home from out of town, the phone rings. He answers it, and immediately you sense that it's bad news.

"What? . . . Yes, officer, I'm the owner of the Morton Electronics plant." There's a pause, then Uncle Sidney gasps. "When was this? Was anything taken? . . . Yes, please let me talk to Bob. . . . Hello, Bob? Thank goodness you're all right! What happened?"

As you watch anger start to cloud your uncle's face, you begin to feel a nagging doubt building inside you. Did you let something awful happen today?

Uncle Sid listens intently, then looks resigned. "And what about the robots?" You freeze, awaiting the answer.

"Oh, no! All of them? . . . The circuit diagrams, too?" Uncle Sid slumps into a chair, almost in shock. "You know what that means, Bob. Now there's no way we can fill that government contract on time. . . ."

When Uncle Sid finally hangs up, he turns and says weakly, "Terry, a terrible thing has happened. There's been a theft at the plant. The robots and their plans have been stolen."

"I know," you reply meekly, with your eyes to the floor.

Stunned, Uncle Sid exclaims, "What do you mean, you know?"

"Well, I didn't really know what was happening at the time, but . . ."

It's as hard as anything you've ever had to do, but you continue.

"Dennis and I went to the plant this morning. We saw Max in the parking lot, even though I thought he was supposed to be in Hawaii. He was using a walkie-talkie or something, and it looked real strange, so we asked him what was going on."

Your uncle's astonishment turns to intense interest. "What did he say?"

"He didn't really say anything, except that you knew he'd be around and that it was none of our business. Then he told us to get lost."

"Well, what did you do? Why didn't you call the police?"

That's the question you hoped he wouldn't ask. "I don't know. Max said he'd have Bob Gladding call me . . . so we just left after that."

You don't have to hear Uncle Sid's words to know his disappointment. Even though he says it's okay, you know it's not. Max lied to you—and you believed him! Now you know that you should have called the police!

That evening, you go with your uncle to the police station to make statements to the detectives and a man from the FBI.

You tell the detectives about seeing Max and about the rental truck, hoping you can help them catch him and whoever was with him. The FBI agent tells you that apparently Max was working with foreign agents who were stealing technology. They got away with all the robot models, computer files, and blueprints.

In only a matter of weeks, Morton Electronics goes out of business. On top of that, Max is never caught and your robot is never seen again. You read in the newspaper that the FBI believes that Max escaped to another country after receiving a big payoff. You feel bad that you helped him get away with it so easily. You vow that someday, when you're older, you'll track him down and bring him to justice, no matter what it takes.

THE END

Max grabs you and pulls you toward one of the workbenches. The other man grabs Dennis and does the same.

"You won't get away with this!" you say.

"Oh, yeah? Why not?" Max asks, surprised.

"Because people like you never do! You're just a big loser, Max!"

Max is angry now. "Your uncle and that fool Gladding had their chance. Now it's my turn. I've got the robots now, and they'll never see 'em again."

Dennis can't hold back any longer, either. "You're a jerk, Max! You'll get caught right away."

"What makes you so sure?"

"We know everything," you tell him. "We know you're smuggling the robots by air freight. When we tell the FBI, they'll put you in jail till you rot!"

Now Max is enraged. He grabs you by the shirt and yanks you toward him. "No stupid kids are going to stop me! You two just bought a one-way plane ride because you couldn't keep your mouths shut."

"What do you mean?" you ask.

"You're gonna get to fly along with your robot friends, kid. Only it gets pretty cold at forty thousand feet in the belly of a cargo jet! Like I said, it's a one-way trip!" With that, he pushes you onto the floor. "Tie 'em up!" he tells the other man.

Please turn to page 20.

"Follow me!" you tell Dennis and sprint off toward the research lab where Bert, your robot, is stored. Dennis and Rusty follow closely as you dash between tall piles of storage boxes.

The door to the lab is open and the light is on, but no one seems to be around. The desk and work area are a mess, as if someone had been rummaging through them. But there in the corner stands Bert. Suddenly you hear boxes falling outside the door. Is it Max?

"Now what, Terry?" Dennis asks.

"Get ready," you tell him. "If that is Max and he comes in here, we'll have to move fast." You pull Bert's controller unit out of your pocket.

"Will it work?" asks Dennis.

You press a button. Bert comes to life with a whirring noise. Dennis jumps, surprised. Rusty is startled, too, and begins to growl deep in his throat.

"Shhh!" you tell Rusty, but you're too late. Max is there in the doorway. He glares and starts to come toward you. Dennis backs off to the side, but Rusty holds his ground and continues to growl.

There is hatred in Max's eyes as he stalks toward you. "I told you to get lost, kid, and I meant it!" You've seen Max angry before, but never like this.

"Stay back, Max!" you shout, doing your best to sound braver than you feel. You press a button and Bert moves forward.

Once more Dennis and Rusty give a start as the strange mechanical thing responds to your command.

Max continues to advance, one slow step at a time. "Don't do anything stupid, Terry. You know I'm not afraid of that piece of junk of yours."

You step back, trying to escape his menacing eyes.

"Terry," Max says, "you're a smart kid. Don't try anything dumb. Now, just give me that controller unit." Max holds out his hand and takes another step forward. "We don't want anybody to get hurt, do we?"

Max is almost upon Bert now. Rusty and Dennis seem frozen in place, watching. It's a tense moment, and you've got to make a decision.

1) If you decide to heed Max's warning and give him the controller unit, turn to page 45.

2) If you decide to try to use Bert's Taser device on Max, turn to page 134.

"C'mon!" you urge Dennis, heading for the warehouse door. He and Rusty follow you through the door, off the loading dock, and around the back of the building. Then you head for the nearest busy street, where Dennis is sure you'll find a telephone.

At a corner supermarket, you find a public phone and call the 911 emergency number. You try to be calm as you tell the police dispatcher what you've seen, but it's not easy. She tells you to stay where you are and that a squad car will be sent right away.

Just as you and Dennis come out of the supermarket, a truck zooms around the corner in front of the store. Dennis grabs your arm and shouts, "Terry! It's that rental truck!" You look up and, sure enough, it's the same Express Rental truck that was at the factory! And Max is at the wheel!

"He's getting away!" you yell, almost in a panic. "We've got to stop him!"

But Dennis is one step ahead of you. He's talking with a big burly man in a parking lot. "C'mon, Terry! This guy'll help us!"

As you follow the man to his car, all you can think about is catching Max. This might be your last chance! You and Dennis and Rusty jump into the car and slam the door as the man shifts into gear. "That way!" Dennis shouts excitedly. "He's heading down First Avenue!"

The burly man looks both ways and then hits the gas and pulls out onto the street. You can see the truck about two blocks ahead. "That's it up there!" you tell him.

"Don't worry, kids!" the man tells you as he pulls out to pass a slow-moving car. "Just strap on your seat belts and hold on tight. I used to be a military policeman in the army. There ain't no way he can get away!"

He reaches down and pulls a CB radio transceiver out from under the dashboard. "Breaker, one-nine. This is the King of Clubs speaking. Request police assistance in pursuit of rental truck proceeding north on First Avenue. Do you read me?" You and Dennis look at each other in amazement. He sure picked the right guy to help catch Max!

The reply is quick in coming. "Roger, King of Clubs! This is police mobile unit one-niner. We are heading your way and have requested backup assistance. What is your current location?"

"We are northbound on First Avenue at Caliente Drive. According to the two kids I have with me, the occupants of the truck were involved in a burglary at the Morton Electronics plant."

"Roger, King of Clubs. Our dispatcher has called units to Morton. Keep your eye on the suspects."

"Affirmative. We're gaining on the truck. Are you nearby?"

"Yes, we're almost up to you. We'll take over when the truck is in sight." You and Dennis start looking around, and in a couple of seconds you see the flashing red lights of a patrol car behind you.

"There!" you tell Dennis. "It's the cops!"

Almost at the same moment, another police car appears from a side street, with sirens wailing. Instantly they begin to close in on the truck. Now you've got him!

Max tries to turn down a side street, but still another police car cuts him off. The truck careens into a curb and smashes against a parked car. The police swarm all over the truck with guns drawn, and Max and three other men come out with their hands up. The police are putting the handcuffs on them as you and Dennis pull up and get out of the car.

Max sees you and snarls in frustration, "You! I shoulda known it was you! You wrecked everything!"

You and Dennis watch as Max is taken away by the police. You see one of the patrolmen talking with the man who called himself the King of Clubs. They come over to you and Dennis, and the man stretches out his hand.

"Didn't get a chance to introduce myself, what with all that excitement. The name's Rob Matthews."

A few minutes later, the police take you back to the Morton plant. More police cars and a bunch of reporters have already gathered.

Bob Gladding, Ed, and Milt are talking with the reporters, giving you and Dennis all the credit for rescuing them. The reporters start bombarding you with questions, and the

camera crews take your picture with Dennis,
Rusty, and Rob Matthews.

When things quiet down, the police detectives and a man from the FBI ask you a few
more questions. The FBI man is impressed
with what you've done. Bob Gladding tells
you, "I know your Uncle Sid is going to be
proud of you when he gets back."

When your uncle does come home that
night, he, too, is impressed with how you
saved the robot models and plans. He says
that he wants to help you further your education in electronics. He's going to set up a
scholarship for you to use when you're ready
for college. Twenty-five thousand dollars
seems like an incredible amount of money!
But the best part is his promise to let you come
and work at the Morton Electronics plant
every summer if you want to. It's almost like a
dream come true!

THE END

"Help me get that wire down," you tell Dennis. Working as quietly as you can, the two of you take the first coil off the peg on the wall.

"Find the end and let's see how long this is," Dennis suggests.

"Here it is." You uncoil the wire and wind it around one arm, between your elbow and hand.

"Twenty-four, twenty-five. . . ." You do the math in your head. "At at least two feet per coil, that's around fifty feet. It should be enough!"

"Let's get the other one," Dennis says. The two of you get the other coil down and repeat the process. This time there are only about forty-five feet, but you decide it still seems like enough after double-checking the distance to the ground.

"Play the game again, Dennis. If it's too quiet in here, they might think we're up to something!" Dennis goes back to his game, and soon the air is filled with beeps and buzzes.

You look for a place near the window to anchor the wires. A water pipe along the wall looks like the best bet, so you tie the two wires firmly to it. Then you braid the two wires together. It takes a while, but you finally get to the end.

"Okay, Dennis," you whisper. He leaves his game and joins you.

"Are you ready?" you ask.

"I guess so," he says. "What's the plan?"

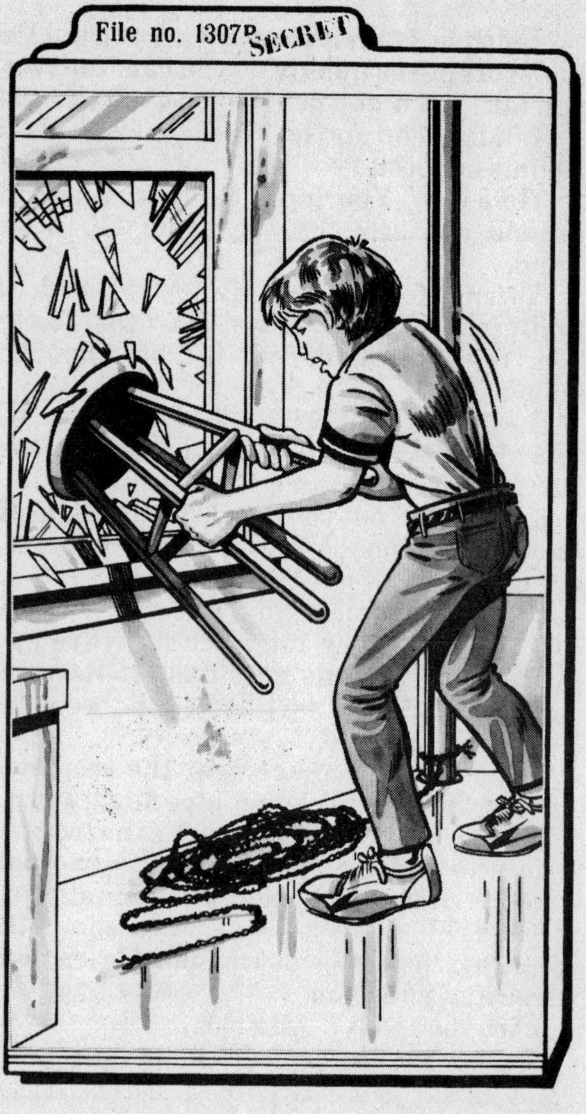
File no. 1307B
SECRET

"The moment I break the window, you push the video games over to block the door. Then we'll lower ourselves out the window and climb down the wire. We should have enough time to get out before they can get in the door, if we're quick enough."

"Okay. Say when."

"Go get in position."

Dennis takes his place by the two Robot Escape games. You grab a wooden stool.

"Now!" you shout.

You swing the stool as Dennis starts to shove the first game across the floor. Even though you hit the window hard, it doesn't break!

It's now or never! You swing the stool again with everything you've got. With a crash, the glass explodes outward. You did it!

Quickly you run the legs of the stool along the edge of the window frame to clear out the shards of glass. Then you drop the stool, grab the braided wire, and toss it out the window.

"Hurry, Terry! They're coming!" Dennis shouts, dashing toward the window. You hear pounding at the door as they try to push it open.

"What's goin' on in there?" Max yells. "I warned you not to try anything!"

You climb onto the window frame, thrust one leg out, and grab the wire with both hands. Suddenly it looks a lot farther down than it did before, but there's no time for doubt now—the door is starting to open! You pull your other leg out and let yourself out the window. The wire is holding!

"Hurry up, Terry!" Dennis shouts, and you lower one hand below the other. You hear a crash as the men push through the door.

Down, down you slide, the slippery wire shooting through your hands. You feel your hands start to burn until it's almost more than you can stand, but then suddenly you're on the ground. You made it!

"Look out, Terry!" Dennis shouts as he zooms toward you. You leap out of the way just as he reaches the ground. "This way!" he shouts and starts to run.

You follow quickly, glancing back up at the window. Max is leaning out, shouting curses at you. As you turn the corner of the building, his voice fades away.

With Dennis in the lead, you run until you find a busy street where there's a phone booth to call the police.

It seems a long time before the police get there. When they finally arrive, you and Dennis lead them to the warehouse. But Max and the others are gone.

When the police hear the whole story, they call for the chief detective and ask for additional cars to be sent. A half hour later, the chief detective arrives with two other men. One of the men introduces himself as an FBI agent, but the other man doesn't say much. As you tell them everything that's happened, the FBI agent questions you about Max.

After you and Dennis have finished answering all the questions, the FBI agent tells you that Max is part of a ring of spies who steal technology from companies all over the world. He says you've provided valuable information about their operations.

As the weeks go by, you wait for word that Max and the other men have been caught, but they never are. Although the robots from the Morton factory are intercepted in Tokyo, the plans are gone forever. You hate to think that a guy like Max could get away with something like this, but apparently he has.

THE END

"No, Dennis!" you exclaim as you grab his arm. "It's too risky! Let's just wait for the police to get here."

Reluctantly Dennis abandons his plan and waits with you. Together you watch as all of the men get into Max's car. One of them carries a large bundle of papers under his arm. They drive off, leaving the rental truck parked at the loading dock.

In about ten minutes, the police arrive, and you tell them everything that's happened. They go inside the building with you and discover Bob Gladding, Ed Segal, and Milt Davis locked up in a storage room. None of the robots have been stolen, but all of the original designs and blueprints are gone.

In a little while, some detectives and a man from the FBI arrive. They question you and Dennis about what you saw. One of the detectives says the two of you were clever in stopping the men from taking the robots, but you know that the missing designs are just as important—and they're gone.

Later, while you're waiting for a ride back to your uncle's house, some TV reporters show up. It's quite a thrill for you and Dennis that evening to see yourselves on the news!

That night, Uncle Sid returns home and learns what's happened. He says that Max may have been working for another company, or even a foreign government. When you ask about the blueprints, he tells you that all the new model drawings were kept in computer storage, and that new blueprints can be made in a couple of days. He says that your preventing the robots from being taken was the most important thing.

After you return home, school starts and you quickly get involved in other things. Then one day when you're home alone, the phone rings. When you answer it, a familiar voice asks, "Is this Terry Morton?"

When you say it is, a chilling reply comes back: "This is Max Kimball, Terry. I know you were the one who stopped us at the Morton plant. I want you to know that you'll never be safe again. Someday, somewhere, somehow, I'm going to get you for what you did. And it won't be pleasant!"

Anger building, you start to reply, but you hear a click and realize no one's listening.

Anger turns to fear as you remember how truly evil Max is. Maybe this time you won't be so lucky. . . .

THE END

"Let's get my robot and finish looking around. Remember, we came here so I could show you how it works!"

"Okay," Dennis agrees reluctantly, "but let's hurry before Max or those other guys get up again!"

You run over to the research lab, where Bert and Gert are kept. The door is open. Papers and electrical parts litter the floor. Someone must have been searching the room!

You take out your hand controller and toss Max's onto one of the tables. By pushing a couple of buttons, you bring Bert to life. With a whir and a series of clicks, he's ready to go. By working the controls, you roll Bert out of the lab and into the assembly area.

Dennis is impressed. "Wow! What a robot! That's better than the ones in the movies!"

You're anxious to show him what your robot can do, but there isn't time. "Let's go to the office area," you tell him. "That's the only place we haven't checked."

With Bert in the lead and Rusty trailing along behind, you and Dennis make your way to the other end of the building. At first it looks as if no one's around. But then, as you move farther down the hallway, you notice that one of the doors is open. It's the blueprint room!

Silently, you point out the open door to Dennis and move your robot toward the doorway. As you follow Bert to a position where you can see through the doorway, you are startled to see the surprised face of a man looking out at the robot! When he sees you, he reaches into his coat!

Afraid that he's reaching for a gun, you frantically press the button to make Bert advance. You see a metallic flash as the man pulls his hand from his pocket. Almost without thinking, you press Bert's Taser control button.

BUZZZZZ!

The man freezes in place, then crumples to the floor with a glazed look in his eyes. The gun clatters to the floor, and Dennis quickly kicks it away.

"Hurry! Call the police!" you tell him. "Use the one on the bridge if none of the other phones work!"

"Gotcha, Terry! I'll be right back. Be careful!" And Dennis dashes out of the room.

As you wait nervously for Dennis to return, you watch the man on the floor, but he doesn't move. You let your eyes take in the rest of the room. It's obvious that he was searching for the plans for the robots, because several early versions are on the table. A tiny camera sits on top of the pile of blueprints. When you look closer, you see that it's unlike any camera you've ever seen.

Soon after Dennis returns, the Morton plant is swarming with police and detectives. You tell them what happened, and they ask you a lot of questions. You have to repeat yourself several times before they get the whole story straight.

You watch as the police handcuff Max and the three men and take them away. It feels good to know that you and Dennis kept them from stealing the robots and the plans.

The next day, your picture is in the newspaper along with a full story about what happened. Your uncle is so grateful that he rewards you and Dennis with ten thousand dollars each, to be set aside for college

When you return to your own home the next week, you find out that there has also been a story about you in your local newspaper. When classes start, the kids at school want to hear the whole story. Suddenly you find it easier to make new friends. . . .

THE END

You stay out of sight and watch Max for a minute more. He keeps looking around nervously in all directions. From time to time, he bends his head, maybe to speak into his walkie-talkie.

Moving carefully, you crouch down to keep the landscaped embankment between you and Max so that he doesn't see you. As you survey the building, you see no signs of any activity. Everything is quiet. No one comes or goes, and the only things you see are Max and the rental truck.

You're wondering what to do next when Dennis grabs your arm and says, "Hey, Terry, take a look at the back of the truck. I think there's enough room between it and the door of the loading dock to squeeze through and sneak into the building without Max seeing us."

"Right! Let's go!"

Trying to keep hidden from Max's view, you lead the way in a low, crouching run, with Dennis and Rusty close behind you. You reach the truck safely and stop for a moment to listen.

Everything is silent, except your heart, which seems to be pounding a mile a minute. You sneak a quick peek through the narrow gap between the truck and the doorway. There's no one in sight in the warehouse. It's now or never.

"C'mon," you whisper to Dennis as you lift yourself up onto the dock and squeeze through the opening. Dennis lifts Rusty up, then follows.

"Wow!" Dennis says in a whisper. "This is a big place!"

"Yeah. During the week it's full of people, but it's kind of creepy with no one around."

Dennis takes a position to serve as a lookout into the warehouse area. You quickly explore the back of the truck, but you see only a few empty boxes.

"Well, this truck certainly looks empty," you tell Dennis.

"What else is located in this building?" Dennis asks curiously.

"There're three sections. The warehouse is where all the finished stuff is stored in cartons and prepared for shipping. The manufacturing area is where the assembly lines and robot lab are located. The third part is the office area, which has the room where all the robot blueprints are kept, my uncle Sid's office, the cafeteria, the library, and a lot of other offices. That's way on the other end."

"Where are the guards?"

"Well, they have an office by the main entrance to the lobby, but usually one of them sits back here where he can keep an eye on the loading dock."

You point to an office chair near the doorway. "Hey, look! That chair's been knocked over!"

"How strange!" says Dennis. "I wonder if something's going on."

"I don't know, Terry. This doesn't look too good. Maybe we should just leave and call the cops."

1) If you want to check around the warehouse to see if anyone is in the shipping or storage area, turn to page 15.

2) If you decide that you'd better call the police instead of getting involved further, turn to page 22.

3) If you want to go to the manufacturing part of the building, where the robot lab is located, turn to page 141.

4) If you want to go to the office area of the building, where your uncle's office and the room with the robot blueprints are, turn to page 16.

5) If you want to call out for the guards, Milt and Ed, turn to page 148.

Max pushes you to the floor on the other side of the room. The second man grabs Dennis and gets the coil of electrical wire from the wall. You look at Dennis, and you can see that he's as scared as you are.

Holding you while the other man ties the two of you together back to back, Max says, "You kids were real smart not to try anything. Now you can just sit back and wait while we take a little trip with the robots."

He pulls the wire tightly around you and stuffs a rag in your mouth. He says, "I hope somebody finds you . . . someday!" And he leaves, chuckling.

You and Dennis struggle against your bonds, but they're so tight there's no way you can get free. You can't even talk to each other because of the rags stuffed in your mouths.

The hours drag on and on, and you get stiffer and sorer as time goes by. You feel Dennis squirming and know that he's just as uncomfortable as you are.

Darkness falls, and soon the only thing you can think of is your growing hunger. You doze for a while, but the growling of your stomach wakes you.

Questions without answers flood your mind. Is Uncle Sid looking for you? Did Rusty make it back? Is anyone ever going to find you here? You've never felt such loneliness and despair.

The sun rises and warms the room. You haven't felt Dennis move for hours. You begin to wonder if you'll ever get to speak to him again. As the day drags on and night falls, you find it harder and harder to focus your mind on anything.

The stupor into which you've fallen is interrupted as the sun is rising on the second day. Something is disturbing you. You wish it would go away. Then suddenly your mind clears and you see a janitor frantically trying to untie you.

"Call... police," you gasp as he removes the gag from your mouth. He frees you both and goes to the telephone. You're rescued at last! Pain shoots through your arms and legs as you try to move them.

While you wait for the police to come, you and Dennis devour everything in the janitor's lunchbox. Liver sausage sandwiches never tasted so good before! After almost two days of waiting, anything would taste like a feast!

When the police arrive, they ask you about Max and the other men. You tell them everything, but you know it's too late. Max is gone for good, and so are the robots. Now you wish with all your heart that you had at least told Max what you thought of him!

THE END

"Okay," you tell Dennis. "We'll each take one tube. You take this door and I'll take the other one. After I turn the corner, start putting the glue around the edge of your doorway. Then slam your door shut as soon as you hear me close the other one."

"All right, but keep real quiet so they don't hear us."

"I will. I'll tell Rusty to stay right here. It shouldn't take long." Then you add, "Boy, I sure hope this stuff works!"

You tell Rusty to stay, then begin to creep quietly around assembly machines and boxes of parts. When Dennis reaches his door, he signals you that he's ready. Rounding the corner near the other door, you see that it's also open.

You look cautiously into the lab to see the two men searching through drawers and piles of papers. You chuckle inwardly, knowing they have no idea you and Dennis are right outside, ready to trap them!

You remove the cap and squeeze the tube. A yellowish goo oozes out. You've got to hurry if it hardens as fast as Dennis says!

Starting at the bottom of the door, you move the tube along the doorframe. In almost no time, you're ready to spring the trap!

"Tell Max you're going to be sticking around for a while!" you shout as you grab the door. The men turn startled faces toward you as you pull it shut. Almost at the same time, you hear Dennis's door close.

With a shout, the men run to the doors and try to open them. The doors rattle and shake, but the glue holds. At least you know the glue guarantee is good!

When Dennis joins you, you tell him, "We'd better call the police. There's a phone over by Rusty. C'mon!"

Rusty is patiently waiting when you get there. You pat him on the head and pick up the phone, ready to dial. But there's no dial tone!

"Rats!"

"What's the matter?" Dennis asks.

"The line's dead! They must've cut the phone lines," you say as you slam the receiver down.

"Max is going to be coming in here any second looking for us!" Dennis reminds you.

"Yeah, you're right. We've got to think of something."

You both look around quickly for ideas.

"Hey, what about those cartons?" Dennis says, pointing to a tall row of parts boxes near the employees' entrance. "When he comes in that door, I'll push the boxes over on top of him."

"Yeah . . . it might just work! Let's go!"

You start across the manufacturing area, headed for the boxes, when you're stopped by a loud, frighteningly familiar voice. "Hey, you kids! Stop!" You turn and see Max rushing in from the warehouse, not the employees' entrance as you expected! He's coming from the wrong direction!

"Now what, Terry? How do we get him over by the boxes!" Dennis whispers excitedly.

You think fast. Maybe you can fool Max. "Let's try to trick him into thinking the police are coming," you whisper to Dennis.

"It'll never work! We've got to get him to go over by the boxes!"

Certain that you're at his mercy, Max stops at the lab door and tries to open it. You can hear the men on the other side pounding at the door, but it won't budge.

"All right, you kids," Max thunders as he turns and starts toward you, his face red with anger. "This time you've gone too far!"

You've got to decide—now!

1) If you want to try to lure Max to where Dennis can push the boxes onto him, turn to page 138.

2) If you want to try to bluff Max into thinking that the police are on their way, turn to page 71.

"Keep playing that game, Dennis. If it's too quiet in here, they'll think we're up to something." Dennis takes his place at the Robot Escape game, and soon there are plenty of sounds to cover any noise you might make.

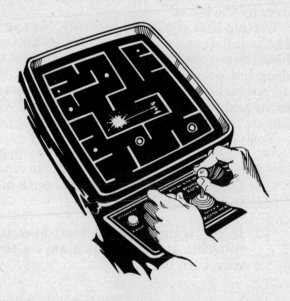

First you remove the cover of the telephone junction box and study the insides. There are lots of wires and connections, but it looks as if you might be able to hook up something, even if you don't have a regular telephone.

From a workbench, you pick up a couple of screwdrivers, a pair of pliers, some clips, wires, connections, and a testing gauge. Then you start to take the back panel off the other Robot Escape game.

"What're you doing?" Dennis asks.

"I'm trying to see if I can get one of the sound units out of here." As you put the back panel aside, you scan the circuit boards inside the game. A small cluster on one side catches your eye. You remove it and take it to the workbench. You examine it and rig up a way to test it for sound.

You remember hearing that the sounds of a video game are like those of a push-button telephone. You explain that to Dennis and add, "Maybe we can tap into the phone line and dial the police."

"But how do we talk to them?" he asks, looking puzzled.

"We can't. But I can send them a message in Morse code."

"How do we hear what they say?"

"We can't. All we can do is send a message and keep repeating it, then hope they pick it up."

"You really think this'll work?"

"Yeah, if we can duplicate a phone's tones and hook it up right."

"Good luck." Dennis shakes his head in bewilderment, then turns back to something he understands better—his Robot Escape game.

You finish connecting the wires to the sound unit and a tiny speaker. Then comes the moment of truth as you test it. You hear a full range of beeps and buzzing sounds. It works!

You practice making beeps in a range of pitches for a few minutes. Then you take your unit over to the telephone junction box and hook it up to the outgoing line.

You take a deep breath and begin to beep out the tones for the 911 emergency number. You slowly count to five, then begin tapping out your message: "S-O-S. C-A-P-T-I-V-E I-N V-I-D-E-O G-A-M-E W-A-R-E-H-O-U-S-E, W-E-S-T S-I-D-E O-F T-O-W-N. S-O-S." It takes a while, but you finally finish. Then you unhook it briefly, reconnect it, and try again.

Dennis has left his game to watch. "Why don't you keep that thing connected? Maybe they can trace the call if you stay on the line long enough," he suggests.

"Good idea!" You send the message again, then repeat it, over and over. Dennis goes back to his game to keep anyone from getting suspicious.

Time drags by. You get tired of tapping out the same message over and over, but you keep on doing it anyway.

After a while, Dennis slaps the side of the video machine and comes over to you. "That's enough of that!" he exclaims. "How's it going?"

"I don't know," you say, discouragement in your voice. "Maybe the signals aren't getting through to anybody."

"Don't give up yet, Terry. It might take them a long time to figure out what building we're in. Don't worry, they'll come." You know

Dennis is trying to be encouraging, but you can tell that he's worried, too. He wanders restlessly over to the window.

"Terry, look! The cops!"

You jump from your stool and dash to the window. Three police cars are pulling up to the building! As the officers pile out, you and Dennis wave your hands to get their attention. One of them sees you and points you out. They gesture for you to stay quiet and then disappear around the corner of the building.

"It worked, Terry! It worked!" Dennis is so happy that he hugs you. You feel pretty proud of yourself . . . until shouts and sounds of men running remind you that you haven't been rescued yet.

You stand still, listening. You hear a series of loud, sharp cracks coming from below. Gunshots! You run to the door and try it, but it's still locked tight. You continue to wait.

In a minute, the door springs open, and two patrolmen burst into the room. You're rescued at last!

When they take you downstairs, you see that Max and the other three men are all in handcuffs. Max glares at you but is strangely silent for a change. The police find the three robots packed inside video game crates. The blueprints are there, too. When you tell them about the break-in at the Morton plant, they send other squads to check it out. They rescue Bob Gladding, Ed Segal, and Milt Davis.

Later a detective and a man from the FBI

arrive. They ask you and Dennis a lot of questions and explain that Max was working with foreign agents to steal robot technology. Thanks to you, their plans have been foiled.

The next day, you and Dennis and Rusty are featured in a front-page newspaper story. It's the first time you've ever been called a hero. Uncle Sid surprises you with a new bike as your reward for stopping Max and the secret agents. What a way to end the summer!

THE END

You know that Max is full of hot air and always tries to threaten people. You're not going to let him push you around! You start to leave, motioning for Dennis to follow.

As you approach the building, you feel Max's eyes on you. Trying to look casual, you stroll right up to the employees' entrance and knock. If the guards are around, one of them will let you in.

No one answers the door, so you pound harder. You don't want to have to walk by Max again. But just as you're about to give up, you hear a shuffling sound inside. Then the lock turns and the door opens.

"Hi," you say, expecting Ed or Milt. Instead, you face two strange men wearing trench coats. They certainly don't look like anyone connected with Morton Electronics!

"What you want, kid?" one asks in a foreign accent. It sounds Russian!

Now you know for sure that something strange is going on here! Your mind spins as you try to decide what to do. . . .

1) If you want to ask these men who they are, turn to page 50.

2) If you want to have Dennis throw his bottle of chemicals at the men, turn to page 68.

3) If you want to run and call the police, turn to page 151.

You look around for something to use to pry open the door. Across the aisle is an open bin with heavy metal rods in it.

"Let's try those," you suggest to Dennis.

"You mean as levers?"

"Yeah. We'll wedge them in around the door and then try to pry it open."

You gather several of the rods and bring them over to the door. As you try to insert the first rod, it's obvious that it is too big to fit between the door and the frame.

Dennis sees your problem and hands you a heavy piece of metal from another bin. "Here, try this as a hammer."

You press the rod up to the crack and start to hammer. There is a loud CLANK! with every blow. You can see that it's working! The rod pushes in a bit farther with every blow. Now if you can just get a few more of them in place to get some leverage. . . .

You grab a second rod, place it over the crack, and start to pound. Just then you hear Dennis scream, "Terry!" and Rusty starts to bark frantically.

You turn quickly and see a man clutching Dennis around the neck with his arm. But before you can react, a hand is cupped over your mouth and one arm is twisted up behind your back. You're helpless!

The man pushes you up against the wall and holds you there while the other man speaks into a walkie-talkie. You hear Max's voice answer, "Hold on to them. I'll be right there." You feel a sickening knot in your stomach as you wonder what's going to happen next.

In a minute Max is there. He glowers at you and mutters something under his breath, but you don't catch it all. The man holding Dennis gives Max a key, and he opens the door to the security storage room. There on the floor are Bob Gladding, Ed Segal, and Milt Davis, tied up and gagged! Their eyes show fear as you and Dennis are pushed into the room.

You and Dennis struggle as the men tie you up with nylon cords, but it's no use. In a matter of minutes, the two of you are lying on the floor with the others. Rusty is put in with you, but his barking is no help. You feel emptiness and fear as the door is closed and locked, trapping the five of you in the room.

The hours drag on, and the wait seems endless. Your muscles become stiff and sore from lack of movement, and hunger gnaws at your stomach. But even worse is the question that keeps running through your mind—has anyone even missed you?

After a while, the hunger becomes unbearable. Rusty, sensing the hopelessness of the situation, stops pacing around the room and lies down to sleep. The wait goes on and on.

It seems like you've been locked in the room for days, when finally the door bursts open and your uncle and several policemen barge through. You've never been so glad to see anyone in your life!

As they untie you, Rusty is beside himself with excitement. When the last rope is loosened, you hug him as he licks your face. What a great feeling to be free at last!

You hungrily gulp down the doughnuts and cartons of milk they bring from the vending machines, and each of you tells your part of the story. The police detectives and a man from the FBI write down the details as they question you.

When all the threads of the story are put together, you learn that Max was apparently working with foreign agents who were interested in stealing technology. Unfortunately, they got away with all the robot models at the plant, as well as the blueprints. Bob Gladding and your Uncle Sid are sick about it.

You find out later that Max has escaped to a foreign country. The robots are never seen again. Over and over again, you find yourself wishing you had done something different to change the way things have worked out.

THE END

Suddenly you're tired of being afraid. Max isn't going to bully anyone anymore. It's time to fight back!

You take a deep breath and press the Taser button on the controller. The dart shoots out from the front of Bert's body and thuds into Max's leg. There's a quick buzzing noise, and Max freezes in place, a look of surprise on his face. He starts to reach out toward you, then collapses to the floor like a tumbled puppet.

"Attaboy, Terry!" Dennis says. "He's a mean one!"

"Good thing it worked. I'd never used the Taser device before." You breathe a sigh of relief when you think about what might have happened if it hadn't functioned.

Dennis goes to the telephone on the wall of the lab, but it won't work. "It's dead!" he says. "Now what?"

1) If you want Dennis to get to a phone and call the police while you stay and keep an eye on Max, turn to page 74.

2) If you want to use Bert's special abilities as a security robot to help you check the rest of the building, turn to page 144.

You don't know what Dennis is up to, but you can't abandon your friend. Rusty follows, puzzled by the strange black contraption in pursuit. You're alarmed at how quickly Bruno is gaining on you!

Dennis turns and heads toward a corner of the assembly area where there's nothing but two towering rows of boxes.

"Not that way, Dennis!" you warn him. "It's a dead end!"

But Dennis doesn't seem to be worried. "Have Rusty hold 'em back for a second," he whispers. "Then we'll go around in back of these boxes and push 'em over on Max and his robot."

It's your only hope. As you reach the end of the aisle, you glance back to see Bruno still approaching, with Max close behind at the controls. He starts to laugh evilly.

"Ha! You kids thought you could get away, didn't ya? Well, it's not gonna be so easy this time! I've got plans for you two, and they're not pretty!"

You can tell he means business. You've got to act fast if you're going to stop him.

"Rusty, stay!" you shout to the dog. He turns and holds his ground, growling deep in his throat.

"Your dog'll be the first to go!" Max threatens. Bruno's claw arm drops lower as it bears down on Rusty.

"Okay . . . now!" you yell to Dennis. Both of you run around the end of the pile of boxes and throw all your weight at it. The boxes lean, start to tip, then finally tumble into the aisle with a thundering crash. All you hear is a muffled cry and the clank of metal as the cartons strike Max and Bruno. The whirring and clicking noises abruptly stop.

As you approach the pile of boxes, you see Rusty off to one side, safe and sound. Max is nowhere in sight, but you hear him groaning underneath the pile. The hand controller lies abandoned on the floor. You pick it up. It looks like Max and his robot are no longer a threat.

"He's not going anywhere!" Dennis says, smiling. "Let's call the cops."

"Wait, Dennis. What if there are more guys around? They'll get away!"

"I think we've pushed our luck enough, Terry."

1) If you want to call the police as Dennis suggested, turn to page 74.

2) But if you want to get your own robot and look for other intruders in the building, turn to page 111.

Quickly you head for the pile of boxes near the door, with Dennis and Rusty right behind you. Max starts to follow and shouts, "Hey, you kids come back here!"

As you near the boxes, you stop running, hoping Max will think you're going to do as he says. Dennis stops, too, then looks back at Max. "Be careful, Terry!" he warns you.

As Max approaches, he glares at you, hatred in his eyes. "You kids've meddled in my plans enough!" he snarls. "But now you're gonna pay for it!"

Rusty starts to growl at Max, but the big man keeps on coming, his attention focused on you. Out of the corner of your eye, you see Dennis slide quietly around the corner of the pile of boxes. This had better work!

Max stalks slowly toward you, his steel-gray eyes fixed on yours. You've never seen anyone look like that, except in a movie. Maybe he's crazy!

"I'm gonna kill you, Terry!" he mutters. He starts to raise his arms, as if to choke you. He IS crazy!

Just then, you hear a grunt from behind the stack of boxes. The pile starts to teeter, and as you look up you can see the uppermost boxes starting to fall. Max has his eyes focused on you and doesn't see the tumbling boxes. At the last instant, you and Rusty jump back out of the way. Too late, Max looks up as the boxes crash down upon him. He disappears under the avalanche of cartons.

Suddenly everything is quiet. Dennis joins you, smiling broadly. "It worked!" he says, slapping you on the back. "We got him!"

"Nice going, Dennis! Now you'd better hurry and call the police. How about using that phone up on the bridge?"

"Okay. Will you be waiting here?"

"Yeah. But hurry up!" Dennis runs out the side door, while you wait behind to keep an eye on Max. You hear an occasional moan from under the pile, but Max certainly isn't going anywhere.

In a few minutes, Dennis comes back with the police. It isn't long before the place is swarming with officers and detectives. They pull Max out from underneath the boxes and put handcuffs on him, then take him away.

Soon two policemen come in, dragging the man you knocked out with Dennis's gas. To get to the other men, the police have to cut a hole in the wall of the research lab. When they search through the rest of the plant, they find Bob Gladding, Milt Davis, and Ed Segal tied up in a storage room and set them free.

The detectives ask lots of questions about what happened, and you and Dennis have to tell your story several times. You notice that one of the men doesn't seem like a policeman. He keeps talking about "the agency," whatever that is. After they're finished with you, you go outside and find that there are TV and newspaper reporters who ask you the same questions all over again!

That night, you and Dennis are on television. Even Rusty recognizes you! The newscaster calls you heroes, and it feels good to be the center of attention.

For some reason, Uncle Sid never thanks you, and that's the most puzzling part of all. In fact, he hardly mentions anything about what happened. He seems worried and distant. Even when you bring up the subject before you leave for home, he says he doesn't want to talk about it.

A couple of weeks after you fly back home, your mom and dad tell you that Uncle Sid has disappeared completely. An FBI agent comes to your house to talk to your father about Uncle Sid, but they talk privately and your dad says he can't ever discuss it with you. It all seems kind of strange, until for some reason you think of the key you saw in the door to Uncle Sid's office. Could Uncle Sid and Max? . . . No, of course not, you decide. Maybe someday you'll know the rest of the story.

THE END

"This way!" you say to Dennis as you start cautiously through the warehouse.

"Where are we going?"

"To the manufacturing area, where the robots are kept. We've got to make sure they're safe."

As you move cautiously through the warehouse, you both look down the empty aisles between rows of boxes. It seems strangely quiet. Does some unseen danger lurk beyond the next row?

You move on, through an open door and into the assembly area.

"Wow!" Dennis whispers. "Is this where they build the robots and other stuff?"

"Yeah. Those are all assembly lines."

Machines and assembly tables fill the large room, and electronic parts are everywhere you look.

"Let's go over there." You point toward the middle of the room. "We can see into the research lab from there. The robots are kept there." The two of you make your way stealthily past looming machinery and piles of metal and plastic parts.

"Listen!" Dennis says softly. You stop and listen. You hear voices!

"Where are they?" Dennis asks.

You raise your head to peer over the top of a machine. Through the doorway to the lab, you can see two men in gray trench coats, looking through cabinets and drawers. Bert stands near the open doorway. That's not where you left him yesterday! The two men are talking, but you can't make out what they're saying.

"They're in the research lab."

Dennis sneaks a glance over the top of the machine and sees the two men also. "What are they doing?"

"They're looking for something. Let's move a little closer."

You make your way stealthily to a well-hidden spot behind an assembly table where you're close enough to get a good look.

You can hear the men speaking into hand-held radios with heavy accents that sound Russian!

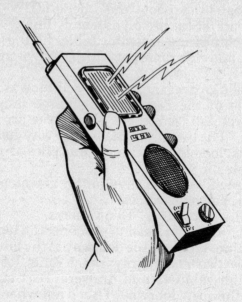

"Max, is just as you said! These will please our superiors very much!"

Max's voice crackles back over the radio. "Good, Yuri! Your people are paying me plenty for this, so be sure to get it all."

"Don't worry. We will. But is time to go soon, yes?"

"Yeah. You'd better hurry it up. Get those robots and let's get rolling!"

1) If you want to stay and observe the two men awhile to find out what they're going to do, turn to page 60.

2) If you want to activate Bert by using your hand controller and use the robot against the men, turn to page 77.

"Let's use the robot to see if anyone else is around. If they're trying to steal the robots, they might go after the computer files and blueprints, too."

"Where are they kept?" Dennis asks.

"Near my uncle's office. That's where the safe is, too. Let's go!"

You press a button and the Taser dart retracts back into Bert's body. With another button, you turn the robot around and guide it out the door. You, Dennis, and Rusty follow a short distance behind.

As Bert glides silently across the floor, you turn on his sensors to find anyone who might be in his detection field. Except for the two men still unconscious by the employees' entrance, the manufacturing area is empty, so you head for the offices.

The door to the office area opens automatically as Bert approaches it. You wait near the company library while Bert sweeps down one corridor past the cafeteria, but nothing is there. Then you turn him around to check near your uncle's office. Dennis just watches in amazement.

All of a sudden, a red light on the controller starts to flash. Bert has found someone! You redirect the robot's detection sensors, trying to locate the source of the body heat that triggered the light. In a second, it's apparent that someone's in your uncle's office! Even though the door to the office is closed, you know there has to be somebody inside.

"Someone's in there!" you whisper to Dennis, pointing to an office door that reads, "SIDNEY MORTON, PRESIDENT."

"How do you know that?" Dennis asks.

"Bert told me," you whisper back.

"Amazing!" Dennis mutters, shaking his head. "Okay. What should we do now?"

"We'll get him when he comes out. We can—"

But there's no chance to finish the sentence, because at that moment the door opens and a man rushes out, straight at Bert.

Bert is turned at too much of an angle to use the Taser device, but the surprised man has stopped dead in his tracks, right in front of the robot's open hand. Quickly you press a button and Bert extends the arm and grabs the man. "Get him!" you shout.

Rusty and Dennis need no encouragement. The dog leaps at the man's leg and grabs it, growling ferociously. Dennis jumps on the man while his attention is on the dog and the robot. Quickly you dash into your uncle's office and grab the first weapon you see—a heavy paperweight. Behind you, you hear a loud metallic clang, and you rush out to see Bert tipped over, his arm still grasping the man.

Dennis sits on top of him, hitting him with his fists, while Rusty chews on his leg. The man tries to fight back, but to no avail. Dennis sees the paperweight in your hand and pulls back to give you an opening. You hesitate an instant, then hit the man on the head with the paperweight, and he slumps, unconscious, to the floor.

"Thanks, Terry," Dennis says. "I was worried about whether we could hold him."

"See if he's got a gun," you say. Dennis feels the man's coat. His hand stops when he finds a lump under the arm. He reaches in and pulls out a shiny black pistol.

Dennis points the gun away from you and pulls hard on the slide action. You see a glint of silver in the chamber. Dennis says solemnly, "And it's loaded. If that guy had drawn his gun, we could have been dead!"

You pick up the phone receiver in your uncle's office to call the police, but there is no dial tone. You tap on the switch hook several times, but the phone is dead.

"This phone is dead, too!" you tell Dennis. "You guard this guy and I'll go call the police from the phone on the bridge."

"Okay, but hurry up! I don't want to have to use this gun on anyone." Fortunately, Dennis knows how to handle guns safely, so you're not worried.

Leaving Rusty with Dennis, you run through the office area and out a side door into the parking lot. When you get to the telephone on the bridge, you dial the 911 emergency number and ask the police to come right away.

The first patrol cars arrive just as the two men start to wake up from the knockout gas. You tell the officers what's happened, and they call for backup units. In a few minutes, the Morton plant is swarming with police.

When the police search the building, they find Max and capture the three men who were working with him. Bob Gladding, Milt Davis, and Ed Segal are discovered locked in a storage room. By that time, television and newspaper reporters are there. You and Dennis get to tell the story all over again. One of the reporters tells you, "By tomorrow morning, kid, your name will known be all over the country."

That night, your Uncle Sid comes home and hears about the whole incident. He tells you that you saved his company by preventing the robots from falling into the wrong hands. As a reward, he gives you and Dennis each two hundred shares of Morton Electronics stock. You know the stock will be worth a lot in a couple of years. Getting rich might not be so bad, you decide!

THE END

Milt and Ed must be here, since their cars are parked outside. You go through the warehouse, calling out loudly, "Hello? Anybody here?" You call several times, and then finally you hear footsteps approaching.

"Milt? Ed?" you call out. Then you realize you've made a big mistake. From behind a pile of boxes step two strange men in trench coats. And they have guns!

"Well! And who have we here?" asks one of them. He speaks with some kind of accent.

The men approach with weapons drawn. They look like secret agents, menacing and evil. What are they up to?

As the men come near, Rusty bares his teeth and growls loudly. One man's gun moves from you and points at your dog. Fear grips you—is he going to shoot Rusty? "Sit, Rusty!" you command. "Sit and stay!" Rusty obeys reluctantly, keeping an eye on both men. The closest man moves his gun off Rusty, then reaches out and grabs you. The other speaks into a hand-held radio. Now you recognize that accent—it's Russian!

"Max, is problem here!"

Max's voice crackles back over the radio. "What is it, Boris?"

The man studies you and Dennis as he continues. "Is two kids here with dog, comrade! What you should want us to do?"

"Tie 'em up and then get rid of the dog! We'll take 'em along with us in case there's any sort of trouble. And put blindfolds on 'em!"

"Is good, comrade!" the man replies. He says something in Russian to his companion, who grabs Dennis by the arm.

Just then a third man comes into the warehouse. He looks just as menacing as the first two. The three talk among themselves in Russian for a minute.

When you try to pull your arm free from the man holding it, he gets angry and points his gun right in your face. He means business! You'd better not try anything for now. Dennis remains silent. You can tell he's as scared as you are.

The men search both of you and take away Dennis's bottle and your robot controller. Then they make you lead Rusty into a room and shut him inside. Next they tie up the two of you. Finally they stuff dirty rags in your mouth so you can't talk.

The men take you and Dennis into the back of the truck and shove you to the floor. For the next few minutes, you watch as the truck is loaded with boxes and equipment. Then the door closes and you're left in silence.

Soon the truck starts to move, and you're on your way. But where?

Please turn to page 37.

"C'mon!" You grab Dennis's arm and start to run. One of the men lunges at you, but Rusty growls and the man hesitates.

Running as fast as you can, you and Dennis round the building into the alley. Two blocks later, you pause to catch your breath. Then you gasp, "We've got to . . . find a phone . . . and call the police!"

Fifteen minutes pass before you find a drugstore with a phone. You dial the 911 emergency number and tell the dispatcher what you've seen. She promises to send a squad car and asks you to stay where you are.

Ten minutes later the police show up and take you to the plant. Max is gone, and so is the rental truck. But the loading dock door is open. The police find Bob Gladding, Ed Segal, and Milt Davis tied up and locked in the storage room. The robot models and all of the blueprints have been stolen.

You tell the police everything you remember, but you never got a good look at the men. You hope you saw enough to help.

Unfortunately, Max is never caught and no trace of the robots ever turns up. Your Uncle Sid tells you you're a hero for reporting the crime, but you don't feel much like a hero. Bert and Gert are gone, and your uncle's company has lost its most important new products. You wonder what would have happened if you hadn't run away. . . .

THE END

As you and Dennis approach Max, you feel his eyes watching your every step. The angry scowl on his face deepens as you approach him.

At your side, Dennis hesitates, tugs your sleeve, and whispers, "Be careful, Terry. He looks mean."

You decide that your best bet is to act as if nothing's wrong.

"Hi, Max," you say, trying to sound casual.

Max ignores your greeting. "What are you doing here?" he demands. His voice is hostile and threatening, just like the time your neighbor, Mr. Hanson, caught you snooping around inside his garage. You feel the same empty feeling in your stomach as you felt then.

You try to relax and not let Max scare you. "We're here to meet Bob in the lab and see Ed and Milt. We're going to run the robots for a few minutes." You hesitate a moment and then ask, "But what are YOU doing here? I thought you were supposed to be in Hawaii."

The scowl on his face deepens. He grabs your arm and says, "Look, kid, I don't answer to your Uncle Sid and I sure don't answer to you! Your uncle knows I'm gonna be here today. Now, just get lost. I'll have Gladding call you later on." Max tightens his grip on your arm, then lets go with a sharp twist.

You clutch your arm in pain. By your side, Rusty growls deep in his throat and shows his teeth.

"C'mon, Terry. Let's go," Dennis whispers nervously. Forgetting the pain in your arm, you think about the choices you have.

1) If you want to follow Max's advice and "get lost," turn to page 92.

2) If you want to ignore Max and go inside the building, turn to page 129.

3) If you want to let Max think you're leaving and then check around the outside of the building, turn to page 31.

"How do you want to do this?" you ask Dennis.

"Well, first we'll tell them we have to go to the bathroom. On the way there, we'll keep an eye out for a second fire extinguisher. Then on the way back, we'll grab both extinguishers and start spraying. Be sure to aim for their faces."

"Think it'll work?"

"I'm pretty sure it will, if we're quick enough."

"Do you have any idea how to use those things?"

"Yeah. You just twist the safety pin hard, to break the seal. Then you point the funnel and give the handle a hard squeeze. They're pretty neat."

"Okay. Let's try it."

Dennis walks over to the door and pounds on it to get someone's attention. At the sound of someone coming, he gives you the thumbs-up signal.

"Whattaya want?" It's Max's voice.

"You guys got a bathroom here?" Dennis asks loudly.

"Okay, okay," Max mutters. You hear the key turning in the door and it opens. As you and Dennis step out of the room, Max points across the office to another door. "It's over there. Make it snappy!"

One of the other men comes along to make sure you don't make a break for it. As you walk you try to look for another fire extinguisher without calling attention to yourself. Finally you see one near the rest room door.

Once you're both inside the bathroom, Dennis whispers, "I'll grab the one on the wall here and you take the one back by our room. Get ready to break for it when I give the signal. Okay?"

You agree, flush the toilet for effect, and open the door. Your guard is leaning against the wall by the door. He watches as you head across the office, then follows at a distance. Slowly the two of you walk back toward the other room. Your heart starts to pound wildly. Then all of a sudden, Dennis yells, "Now!"

Like a flash, you're off across the room. Max and the other men are slow to react, so you get a jump on them.

You yank the extinguisher from the wall. It's heavy! As you clunk it down on the floor, you grab the pin and start to twist it hard. The plastic seal won't break! You tighten your grip and twist it again, as hard as you can. It better work this time. You can hear someone running toward you!

Just when you think your finger is going to break before the plastic does, the seal snaps. You point the funnel upward as you lift the heavy extinguisher. It's not a moment too soon. Max and one of the men are almost upon you!

You breathe a quick prayer and swing the funnel up right at Max's face as he lunges for you. You squeeze the handle, and a white

cloud bellows around Max's head. He falls to the floor, clutching his face. You swing around and spray at the other man. In a second, they're both thrashing on the floor, unable to see or breathe. They're helpless for now, but there's no time to waste!

You spot some electrical wire on a desk. As you grab it, you see that Dennis has also been successful. "Tie them up!" you shout.

"Okay!" he yells back as you start to tie up Max, still too helpless to put up much of a fight. You make sure the wire's good and snug.

When all the men are tied up, Dennis calls the police on a phone in the office. He describes the warehouse, and the dispatcher recognizes the location. In minutes, the police are there.

After the police hear your story, they summon the FBI. Another man arrives to question you. He explains that Max and the other men were stealing robot technology for a foreign government. You kept the robots and blueprints out of the wrong hands.

The next day, the newspaper carries a story about you and Dennis. Then a network TV crew comes to interview the two of you. But the biggest surprise comes when your Uncle Sid gives each of you a home computer system as a reward. It's the best possible ending to your summer!

THE END

ENDLESS QUEST™ Books

From the producers of the
DUNGEONS & DRAGONS® Game

#1 DUNGEON OF DREAD

#2 MOUNTAIN OF MIRRORS

#3 PILLARS OF PENTEGARN

#4 RETURN TO BROOKMERE

#5 REVOLT OF THE DWARVES

**#6 REVENGE OF
THE RAINBOW DRAGONS**

#7 HERO OF WASHINGTON SQUARE
based on the TOP SECRET® Game

#8 VILLAINS OF VOLTURNUS
based on the STAR FRONTIERS™ Game

#9 ROBBERS AND ROBOTS
based on the TOP SECRET® Game

#10 CIRCUS OF FEAR

#11 SPELL OF THE WINTER WIZARD

#12 LIGHT ON QUESTS MOUNTAIN
based on the GAMMA WORLD® Game

For a free catalog, write:
TSR Hobbies, Inc.
P.O. Box 756, Dept. EQB
Lake Geneva, WI 53147

TSR Hobbies, Inc.

The Official Fuel for Over 100,000 of the World's Most Imaginative Gamers

- **DRAGON™ Magazine is a storehouse of information.**

It's the acknowledged leader. No other hobby gaming magazine has the size and circulation.

- **DRAGON™ Magazine is actually a monthly role-playing aid.**

It fuels the best players with ammunition from the best writers. Imaginative articles by the co-creator of DUNGEONS & DRAGONS games, E. Gary Gygax, appear in each issue. Hundreds of authors and games from all manufacturers are featured throughout. And with a cost of only $24 for your year's supply of fuel, it's hard to imagine how you got anywhere without it!

For information write:
Subscription Department, Dragon Publishing
Box 110, C186EQB Lake Geneva, WI 53147

DRAGON™ Magazine
Box 110, C186EQB
Lake Geneva, WI 53147

In the UK:
TSR Hobbies, (UK) Ltd.
The Mill, Rathmore Rd.
Cambridge, ENGLAND
CB1 4AD

TSR Hobbies, Inc.
Products Of Your Imagination™